100
New Testament
Stories for Children

100 New Testament Stories for Children

Retold by Jackie Andrews
Illustrated by Val Biro

AWARD PUBLICATIONS LIMITED

ISBN 978-1-84135-126-1

Copyright © 2003 Award Publications Limited
Illustrations © 2003 Val Biro

Published by Award Publications Limited,
The Old Riding School, The Welbeck Estate,
Worksop, Nottinghamshire, S80 3LR

First published 2003
Second impression 2007

Printed in Malaysia

All rights reserved

Contents

A son for Zacharias and Elizabeth	12
Mary is chosen	14
Mary visits Elizabeth	16
The birth of John the Baptist	18
Baby Jesus	20
Shepherds worship the Saviour	22
Wise men worship the king	24
The holy family returns to Nazareth	26
The boy Jesus in Jerusalem	28
John baptises Jesus	30

Jesus in the desert	32
Jesus calls his first disciples	34
The marriage feast at Cana	36
Jesus in Simon Peter's house	38
The sower	40
Jesus helps a Roman officer	42
Jesus at the house of Simon the Pharisee	44
Jesus tells Simon a story	46
A blind beggar	48
The daughter of Jairus	50
Jesus has no home	52
The ploughman	54
Peter believes in Jesus	56
Jesus rebukes Peter	57
Jesus is transfigured	58
Martha and Mary	60
Talking to God	61
The way to pray	62
Jesus and the woman at the well	64
Beware of greed	66
Leaven in the dough	68
The rich young man	70
Wedding guests	72
Guests for a feast	74
A foolish builder	76
Workers in the vineyard	78
Paying the workers	80
Jesus feeds a crowd	82
The unjust judge	84

Zacchaeus the tax collector	86
The last supper	88
Jesus washes the feet of the disciples	90
Judas plots to betray Jesus	92
In the garden of Gethsemane	94
Judas betrays Jesus	96
Judas is sorry	98
Peter breaks his promise	100
Jesus before King Herod	102
Jesus before the Roman governor	104
Barabbas the robber	106
Pilate gives in	108
Jesus dies on the cross	110
Jesus is taken down from the cross	112

The empty tomb	114
Doubting Thomas	116
The road to Emmaus	118
Jesus appears for the third time	120
The Ascension	122
Peter the leader	124
Pentecost	126
Peter proclaims the Good News	126
The lame man is cured	128
Peter and John are arrested	130
The apostles on trial	132
The stoning of Stephen	134
Philip and the Ethiopian	136
Saul on the road to Damascus	138
Saul becomes a Christian	140
Paul begins his ministry	143
Peter at Jaffa	144
Peter's vision	146

Peter in prison	148
Paul and Barnabas	150
Mark the helper	152
Disagreement about the pagans	154
Silas is chosen	156
Paul meets Timothy	158
A lady named Lydia	160
Paul and Silas in prison	162
Paul and the wise men of Athens	164
Paul at Corinth	166
Paul the tent-maker	168
Paul at Ephesus	170

The riot of the silversmiths	172
A life saved at Troas	174
Paul says goodbye to the Ephesians	176
Paul in Jerusalem	179
Paul saved by a boy	180
Paul a prisoner in Caesarea	182
Paul is brought before King Agrippa	184
Paul sails for Rome	186
Storm at sea	188

Paul gives everyone hope	190
Shipwreck	192
Paul on the island of Malta	194
Paul comes to Rome	196
Paul contacts the Jews of Rome	198
A runaway slave	200
The Roman soldier	202
Faithful to the end	204
Map	206

A son for Zacharias and Elizabeth

In the days when Herod was king of Judaea, there lived a priest called Zacharias, and his wife Elizabeth. They had both been very faithful to the Lord God, and their only sorrow was that in spite of all their prayers, they had no children. In those days, it was very shameful for a married woman to be childless. But now they were both growing old and had given up all hope of having a family.

One day, while Zacharias was serving in the temple and the people were praying outside, an angel appeared by the altar.

"Do not be afraid," the angel said to the terrified Zacharias. "Your prayers have been heard. Your wife, Elizabeth, will have a son and you must call him John. He will be a great joy to you both and he will bring happiness and peace to the world. He will be filled with the Holy Spirit and will bring many of the people of Israel back to the Lord their God."

"How can this be?" asked Zacharias. "My wife and I are too old to have children."

The angel replied, "I am Gabriel. I have been sent by God to bring you this good news. Since you have not believed me, you will be unable to speak until all that I have promised is fulfilled."

The people outside were wondering why Zacharias was taking so long. When he came out at last, they knew at once that he had received a vision. But Zacharias, unable to speak, could not tell them what had happened.

Not long after this Elizabeth became pregnant, just as the angel had promised. She stayed quietly at home, rejoicing and praising God for his mercy. "The Lord has done this for me," she said, "and has taken away my shame."

Mary is chosen

Elizabeth was in the sixth month of her pregnancy when the angel Gabriel was sent to a small town in Galilee called Nazareth. Here there lived a young woman called Mary. She was engaged to be married to a man called Joseph who came from a family descended from King David.

The angel greeted Mary. "Rejoice, Mary, for you are the most fortunate of all women."

Mary was very disturbed by Gabriel's visit and wondered what his strange greeting could mean.

"Do not be afraid," said Gabriel. "I have been sent by God to tell you that you are going to have a son and you must call him Jesus. He will be very great and will be called the Son of the Most High. God will give him the throne of David and he will rule over the people of Israel for ever."

"How can this happen?" asked Mary. "I am still a girl, and unmarried."

"The Holy Spirit will come to you," said the angel, "and the power of the Lord will cover you. The child will be holy and called the Son of God. Your cousin Elizabeth is also going to have a son, even though she is old now, for nothing is impossible to God."

"I am the Lord's faithful servant," said Mary. "Let what you have said be done to me."

And then the angel left her.

Mary visits Elizabeth

Mary set out and went as quickly as she could to the hill country of Judah to visit her cousin. She went into Zacharias's house and greeted Elizabeth.

As soon as Elizabeth heard Mary's greeting, the baby in her womb leaped for joy and Elizabeth was filled with the Holy Spirit.

"You are the most blessed of all women, and blessed is the baby you carry," cried Elizabeth. "Why should I be honoured by a visit from the mother of my Lord? As soon as I heard your voice, the child in my womb leaped for joy. Yes, blessed are you for believing that the promise made to you would be fulfilled!"

Then Mary sang a joyful song of praise to God:

> *My soul proclaims the greatness of the Lord*
> *And my spirit rejoices in the Lord my saviour.*
> *He has looked upon his lowly handmaid.*
> *From this day forward all generations will call me blessed,*
> *For the Almighty has done great things for me.*
> *Holy is his name.*

*His love extends from age to age to all those who
 love and obey him.
He has shown the power of his arm to scatter
 those with proud hearts.
He has pulled down princes from their thrones
 and lifted up the humble.
He has filled the starving with good things,
 but sent the rich away empty.
He has come to the help of his servant Israel
 remembering his mercy,
The mercy promised our ancestors,
To Abraham and his descendants for ever.*

Mary stayed about three months with Elizabeth, and then returned home.

The birth of John the Baptist

The time came for Elizabeth to have her baby, and she gave birth to a son. When her friends and relatives heard the news, they shared her great happiness and praised God for showing her such a kindness.

Eight days later, it was time for their son to be presented in the temple and given a name.

"He must be called Zacharias, after his father," said their relatives.

"No," said Elizabeth, "his name is John."

"But no one in your family has that name," they said.

Then they turned to Zacharias, to see what he thought about it all. Zacharias still could not speak, so he called for a writing-tablet and wrote down, "His name is John." Everyone was astonished.

From that moment, Zacharias was able to speak again and he praised God.

The story of what had happened soon spread throughout Judaea, so that everyone wondered just what this child would turn out to be. Clearly, he was blessed by God.

Then his father, Zacharias, was filled with the Holy Spirit and said:

*You, little child, shall be called Prophet of the
Most High,
     For you will go ahead of the Lord
To prepare a way for him.
     To give his people knowledge of salvation
Through the forgiveness of their sins.*

And the child, John, grew up and lived alone in the desert wilderness until the time came for him to do God's work among the people of Israel.

Baby Jesus

When Joseph learned that Mary was already expecting a baby, being a good man he decided he should quietly release her from their engagement, so that there would be no public scandal. But an angel came to him in a dream and said, "Joseph, do not be afraid to make Mary your wife. The child she carries is from God. She will have a son and you must call him Jesus."

When Joseph woke up he believed everything the angel had told him, and he and Mary were married.

Not long after this, the Roman Emperor passed a law that every person in the empire should be counted.

Each man had to return to the town of his birth, with his family. Joseph and Mary – who was due to have her baby – had to make their way to the town of Bethlehem.

The city was already crowded with people. Leading the donkey that carried Mary, Joseph searched for somewhere to stay, but everywhere was full. Then one innkeeper offered them his stable.

Joseph made Mary a bed in the straw and that night her baby was born. She wrapped him in strips of cloth, called "swaddling", and laid him in a manger where hay was kept for the animals – the only bed in Bethlehem for the Son of God. They called their baby Jesus, just as the angel had told them.

Shepherds worship the Saviour

In the hills above the town of Bethlehem, there were some shepherds looking after their flocks of sheep, making sure they were safe from wild animals such as wolves and jackals.

Suddenly, the sky overhead was filled with dazzling light. The frightened shepherds heard a voice saying, "Do not be afraid! I bring you joyful news. Today, in Bethlehem, the Saviour is born. You will find him there, lying in a manger!"

Then the shepherds heard beautiful voices singing. A host of angels filled the sky, all singing and praising God:

> *Glory be to God in the highest heaven*
> *And peace to his people on earth!*

When the angels disappeared, the shepherds turned to each other in amazement. What was this marvellous thing they had all seen?

"Let's go down to Bethlehem," they said, "and find out what it all means!"

So they left their sheep safely in the stone fold and went down the hillside, into the town. There they found the stable, with Mary and Joseph and their new-born baby lying in a manger, just as the angel had said.

Amazed, the shepherds returned to their sheep, rejoicing and praising God for all the marvels they had seen that night.

Wise men worship the king

After Jesus had been born in Bethlehem some men arrived in Jerusalem, having travelled from far away in the East. They were looking for a very special baby. From their studies of the stars they knew that something very important had happened: there was a new star in the heavens and this meant that a child had been born that was destined to be king of the Jews.

First, they called on King Herod. "Where is the infant king of the Jews?" they asked Herod. "We have seen his star in the heavens and have come to pay him homage."

Herod was not at all pleased to learn that another king had been born – someone who might well try and take the kingship from himself! He discussed the matter privately with the Jewish leaders, who were also very disturbed by the news. "Where will this Christ be born?" he asked them, and they told him that the prophet Micah foretold that the Messiah would be born in Bethlehem, in Judaea.

Herod told the wise men to come back and see him once they had found what they were looking for. "So that I might worship the new king as well!" he said.

So the men continued their journey and followed the star all the way to Bethlehem. There they found the baby Jesus with Mary and Joseph. The wise men presented Jesus with three special gifts: gold because he was a king, frankincense because he came from God, and myrrh because he would suffer and die.

Warned in a dream not to go back to Herod, the wise men returned home by a different route, taking with them the wonderful news that the Saviour of the world had been born and that they had seen him for themselves.

The holy family returns to Nazareth

Not long after the wise men had left, an angel appeared to Joseph in a dream.

"Hurry, take the child and his mother to Egypt," said the angel. "Herod's men are searching for the child. They will kill him if they find him."

Joseph immediately took his family away to Egypt where they would be safe.

In the meantime, Herod was very angry when he realised the wise men had tricked him. He sent his

soldiers out into the region around Bethlehem with the order to kill every boy child under the age of two.

It was not long after this that Herod himself died. Once more an angel came to Joseph in a dream and told him that it would be safe for him to return home. Joseph took Mary and Jesus to Nazareth, in Galilee, where they made a home for themselves and Joseph worked as a carpenter.

Here it was that the young Jesus grew up in the knowledge and love of God. Everyone liked him, and God, his heavenly Father, was very pleased with him.

The boy Jesus in Jerusalem

It was the custom in those days for Jewish families to go up to the temple in Jerusalem every year for the great festival called Passover. When Jesus was twelve, Joseph and Mary took him with them.

When the celebrations were over, everyone set off for home. Mary and Joseph had been travelling for a day when they realised that Jesus was not with their friends or relatives. They went back to Jerusalem to look for him, and searched the city for three days.

They found him in the temple, surrounded by the priests and the teachers of the law, listening to them and asking them questions. These learned men were amazed at his wisdom and intelligence.

"My child," said Mary, overcome with emotion, "how could you do this to us? Your father and I have been so worried about you."

"Didn't you realise I would be in my Father's house?" asked Jesus, but his parents did not understand him.

Jesus returned home to Nazareth and lived obediently with them until the time came for him to do the work of his heavenly Father.

John baptises Jesus

John the Baptist lived alone in the desert wilderness dressed only in camel skins. For food, he ate wild honey and insects such as locusts. Everyone knew he had given his life to God, and they flocked to see him and listen to him preach.

John's message was simple: he urged his listeners to be sorry for all the things they had done wrong in their lives and to turn back to God for forgiveness.

Hundreds of people came to confess their sins, and John would baptise them in the River Jordan as a sign they had repented.

"I baptise you with water," he told them, "but there is one coming after me who will be far greater. He will baptise you with the Holy Spirit. He is so holy that I am not worthy to even undo his sandals. I am preparing the way for him."

One day, Jesus also came to John to be baptised. As soon as he saw him, John said, "It is not right that I should be baptising you: it is you who should baptise me!"

But Jesus replied, "Let it be this way for now. It is what God wants."

He walked into the river with John and as soon as he had been baptised, the Holy Spirit appeared from heaven in the form of a dove and hovered over his head. The voice of God said, "This is my beloved Son, with whom I am well pleased."

Jesus in the desert

After Jesus had been baptised by John, the Holy Spirit led him into the desert to prepare himself for the work ahead of him. For forty days he fasted and prayed, and at the end of this time he was exhausted and hungry. It was then that Satan – the great enemy of God – came to tempt him.

"If you really are the Son of God," said Satan, "why don't you turn these stones into bread and eat it?"

Jesus replied, "Scripture tells us we cannot live on bread alone, we also need the nourishment of God's word."

Satan then took Jesus to a high mountain from which could be seen all the kingdoms of the world.

"Worship me and I will give you power over all these lands," he said.

But Jesus replied, "Scripture tells us we must only worship the Lord our God."

Finally Satan led Jesus to Jerusalem and made him stand on the parapet of the temple. "If you are the Son of God," he said, "throw yourself from this parapet, for scripture says: 'He will put his angels in charge of you to guard you.'"

Jesus replied, "It also says: 'You must not put the Lord your God to the test.'"

Knowing he was defeated, Satan left him.

God then sent his angels to Jesus to look after him and bring him food.

Jesus calls his first disciples

After his time in the desert, Jesus went down into Galilee to begin his mission to tell people all about the coming of God's kingdom. Walking along the shores of Lake Galilee, he saw two boats moored. Jesus stepped into one boat, which happened to belong to Simon and his brother, Andrew. He asked them to take him out a little from the shore. Then he sat down and taught the crowds that had followed him.

When he had finished speaking, Jesus told Simon to take the boat out into deeper water and throw out their fishing net. "Master," said Simon, "we've been working all night, but have caught nothing. However, if you want me to, I'll do as you say."

So Simon and Andrew took the boat out once more and cast their fishing net into the sea, just as Jesus had instructed them. Immediately, they caught so many fish that their net was too heavy to pull into the boat. Their friends, James and his brother John, had to bring their boat over to help them.

After they had struggled to haul in their miraculous catch, Simon fell at the feet of Jesus. He was completely overwhelmed by what had happened.

"Leave me, Lord," he said, "for I am a sinful man."

"Do not be afraid," said Jesus. "From now on you will be fishers of men."

At these words, all four men immediately left everything – even their boats full of fish – in order to follow Jesus.

The marriage feast at Cana

One day, Jesus was invited with his mother, Mary, and his disciples to a wedding at Cana. During the feast, Mary noticed that the wine was running out. Soon there would be nothing for the wedding guests to drink!

Mary told Jesus. "Please do something," she said to him, "or the feast will be spoiled and the bridegroom and his family will be embarrassed."

Jesus reminded his mother that the time to do his heavenly Father's work had not yet arrived, but Mary was sure he would help. She called the stewards over.

"Just do whatever he tells you," she told them.

It was the custom in those days for guests to wash themselves before an important meal, and large jars of water were provided for them to use as they came in the house. Jesus noticed the row of six large water jars standing against the wall: each could hold about twenty or thirty gallons.

"Fill these jars with water," he told the servants. They quickly filled them all to the brim. "Now pour some out and take it to the wine steward to taste," he said.

They did as he said. The wine steward tasted the water and it had turned into delicious wine!

"I see you've left the best wine until last!" he said to the bridegroom. Of course, he had no idea where it had come from.

This was the first miracle Jesus performed, and it showed his disciples that he was indeed from God.

Jesus in Simon Peter's house

Jesus went down to Capernaum, on the shore of the Sea of Galilee, and began teaching people about the kingdom of God. Capernaum was an important, busy town, with a garrison of Roman soldiers and a tax office. Many traders and travellers would have passed through it, and from here Jesus was able to go out to the other towns and villages of Galilee.

Capernaum was also the home of Simon Peter. He and his wife had a house which they shared with his mother-in-law. Jesus probably stayed here at times.

Jesus used to teach in the synagogue, where everyone who heard him was impressed because he spoke with great authority. One Sabbath Jesus healed a man with a troubled mind, and the people were astonished at his power. They began to talk about him and word spread all round the surrounding countryside.

That day, after the service, Simon Peter took Jesus back to his house for dinner. When they arrived, they discovered that Simon Peter's mother-in-law was in bed, very ill with a fever. At once, Jesus was asked to help her.

Jesus stood over her and commanded the fever to leave her. Immediately it went, and she was able to get up and go back to preparing the dinner for them all.

That evening there was no peace in Peter's house. The fame of Jesus had spread, so that by sunset a crowd of people turned up outside the house. They were all suffering in some way or another and came for healing.

Jesus did not send them away but laid his hands on each of them and cured them.

Early next morning, Jesus left the house to find a quiet place to pray. But the crowds followed him and tried to persuade him to stay with them. "No," he said. "I must proclaim the kingdom of God to others, too, for that is what I was sent to do."

The sower

One day, Jesus asked the crowds to imagine a farmer going out to sow seed in his field. The farmer scattered seed by hand as he walked up and down his field. "As the farmer sowed," said Jesus, "some seed fell on the path, and the birds flew down and ate it. Some fell on to rocky ground where there wasn't much soil. It grew quickly, then shrivelled and died in the scorching sun. Some seed fell into thorns which grew up and choked it. But some seed fell into rich soil and grew tall and strong, producing a good harvest.

"The seed is the Word of God. Some people hear the Word, but the Devil hardens their hearts and they soon forget what they have heard. Some hearts are too shallow, like rocky ground; the Word is heard with joy at first, but it does not last. Others hear the Word but are more interested in worldly things, like becoming rich, and the Word is choked like the seed amongst the thorns. But some people hear the Word and accept it, giving a rich harvest of faith, goodness and love."

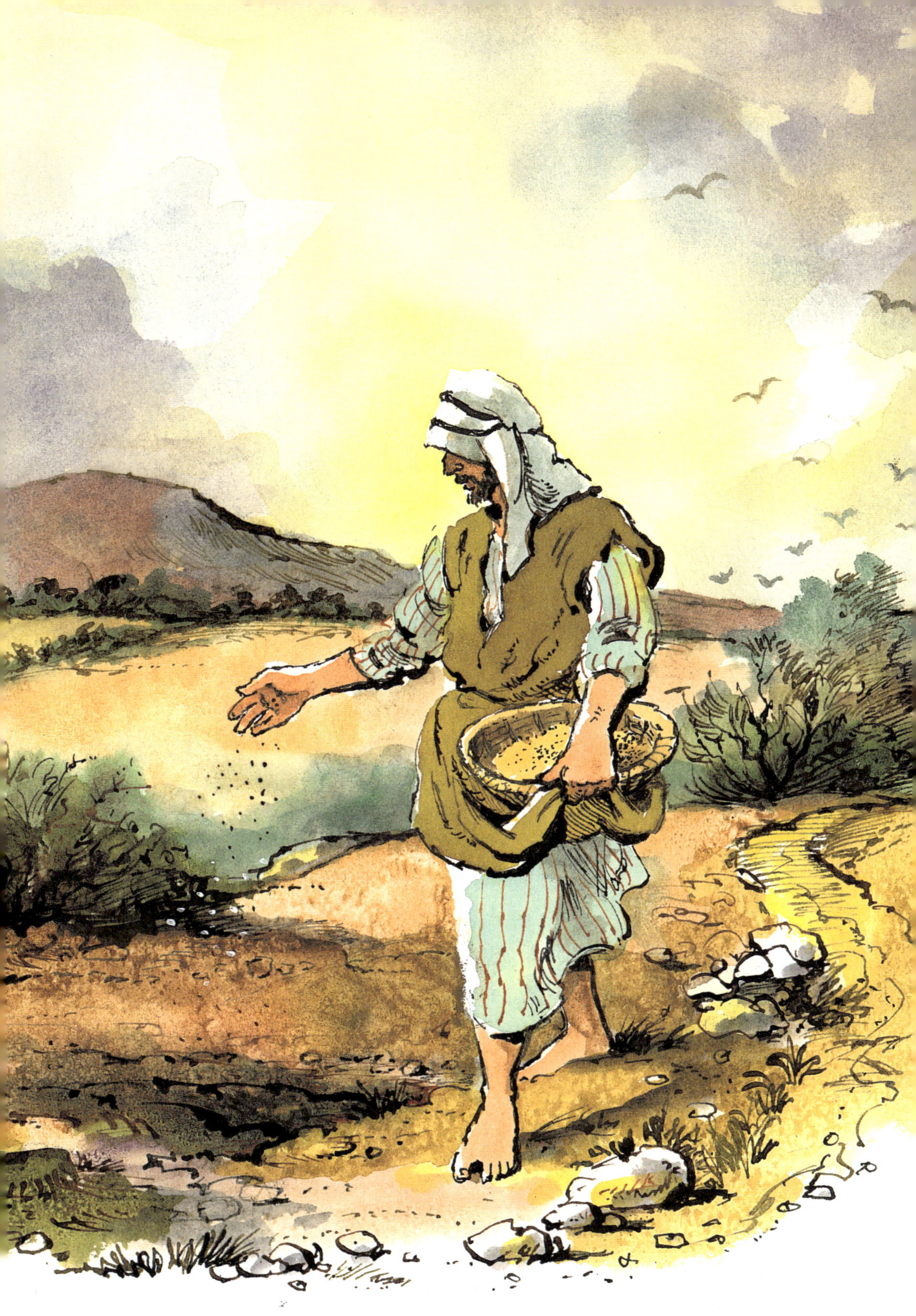

Jesus helps a Roman officer

As Jesus made his way to Capernaum, he was met by some senior Jewish people of the town. One of the Roman officers of the garrison there – a centurion – had asked them to approach Jesus on his behalf. One of his most valued servants was dangerously ill, and the centurion believed Jesus would be able to heal him. He was not a Jew, however, so he did not want to risk offending Jesus by approaching him directly.

The Jewish elders pleaded with Jesus. "He deserves your help," they said, "because he is very good to our people. In fact, he built the synagogue for us."

Jesus went with them to the centurion's house. They were not very far from the house, however, when some of the centurion's friends met them with a message for Jesus:

"Sir, do not put yourself to any trouble for me. I am not worthy enough for you to enter my house, and for this reason I did not come to you myself. Please just say the word and my servant will be healed. For, like you, I have authority: I only have to say to one of my soldiers, 'Go!' and he goes, or 'Come here!' and he comes."

When Jesus heard the centurion's message, he was astonished. He turned to the crowd of people following him and said, "Not in the whole of Israel have I come across faith such as this."

The messengers returned to the centurion's house and found his servant completely healed.

Jesus at the house of Simon the Pharisee

While Jesus was in a town called Nain, one of the leading Jewish men there – a man called Simon – invited him to his fine house for a meal. Simon was a Pharisee, which meant that he lived very strictly according to Jewish law. Jesus, however, was a friend to everyone – rich or poor, alike.

There were a number of customs usual in those days when a guest went to someone's house. The guest would be greeted with a kiss of friendship. His feet would be washed and perfumed oil offered to freshen his face and hair. Simon, however, did none of these things when Jesus arrived at his house.

As a Pharisee, he was anxious to show just the right amount of honour in front of his other guests. He thought that despite what people were saying, Jesus might not be a true prophet of God, after all.

When Jesus took his place at the table, something unusual happened. A woman came quietly into the room, unnoticed by anyone, carrying a jar of expensive ointment. She knelt behind Jesus, at his feet, crying softly. Her tears fell on his feet and she wiped them away with her hair. Then she covered his feet with kisses and spread the perfumed ointment over them with her hands.

Simon watched all of this happening and wondered what he should do about it. The woman had a bad reputation in the town. "Surely, if Jesus really was a prophet," thought Simon, "he would know what a bad name she has and would not let her touch him?"

Jesus, however, knew just what Simon was thinking.

Jesus tells Simon a story

Jesus turned to Simon: "Simon, I have something to say to you," he said.

"What is it, Master?" said Simon, graciously.

"There were once two men who owed a moneylender some money. One man owed him five hundred silver coins. The other owed him fifty. Both of them were unable to pay the moneylender back, so he cancelled both their debts. Which of those two men do you think would be most grateful?"

"I suppose," said Simon, "the one who owed him the most."

"That's right," said Jesus. Then he turned to the woman at his feet.

"Simon, you see this woman, kneeling at my feet? When I came into your house you did not pour any water over my feet to wash the dust from them, but she has poured her tears over them and wiped them away with her hair. You did not greet me with a kiss of friendship, but she has been covering my feet with her kisses ever since I arrived. You did not anoint my head with oil, but she has anointed my feet with perfumed ointment. For this reason I tell you that her sins – her many sins – must have been forgiven, or she would not have shown me such love."

Then Jesus said to the woman, "Your sins are forgiven."

When they heard this, Simon and the other men at the table began to murmur to each other.

"How can this man forgive sins?" they said. "Who is he?"

But Jesus said to the woman, "Go in peace. Your faith has saved you."

A blind beggar

Jesus and his disciples visited the town of Jericho and a large crowd followed them to hear his teaching. As they left the town, they passed a blind beggar called Bartimaeus sitting at the side of the road, begging.

"What's going on?" asked Bartimaeus. He could hear the noise of the crowd.

"It's Jesus, the man from Nazareth, with a crowd of followers," someone told him.

Bartimaeus had heard of Jesus and how he could heal people. He began to shout as loudly as he could, hoping Jesus would hear him. "Jesus! Son of David! Have pity on me!" The people near him told him to be quiet, but Bartimaeus only shouted louder. "Son of David! Have pity on me!"

"Bring him to me," Jesus said to the people nearby.

"Come, get up," they said to Bartimaeus. "Jesus is calling you." Bartimaeus threw off his cloak, jumped up and made his way over to Jesus.

"What do you want me to do for you?" asked Jesus.

"Master," said Bartimaeus, "please let me see again."

"Go," said Jesus. "Your faith has saved you."

Immediately, Bartimaeus could see again and from that moment he became a faithful follower of Jesus.

The daughter of Jairus

One day, a man pushed through the crowd that had come to hear Jesus and threw himself at Jesus' feet. The man was a minister at the local synagogue.

"Master, please help me," he sobbed. "My little girl is very ill. She's dying. She's only twelve years old, Lord. Please come and make her better."

"I'll come at once," said Jesus. But first, he and his disciples had to work their way slowly through the hundreds of people pressing all round them.

They were not far from the house of Jairus when a friend of his met them.

"Your daughter has died," he told Jairus, "so there is no need to trouble the Master any further."

But when Jesus heard this, he said to Jairus, "Don't be afraid. Have faith and she will be safe."

The house was crowded with mourners, weeping and

wailing. Jesus made his way past them to the room where the little girl lay, taking with him only Peter, John and James, and the child's parents.

"There is no need for you to cry," he told the crowd. "The child is only asleep." But they all laughed at him. They had seen for themselves that she was dead.

Jesus stood by the bed and took the little girl's hand. "Come, child," he said. "It's time to get up." At once her spirit returned and she sat up, smiling. "Give her something to eat," said Jesus to her astonished parents. "And don't tell anyone what has happened today."

Jesus has no home

As Jesus travelled through the towns and villages of Galilee with his disciples, spreading the Good News of the kingdom of God, many people flocked to hear him teach and ask him for healing.

But they did not stay for long. Jesus knew that their commitment to God was not strong. Only a few were able to give up everything to follow him and share in his work of teaching and spreading the kingdom of God. It was a hard, demanding life.

One day Jesus was stopped on the road by a man, who said to him, "I want to be your disciple. I will follow you wherever you go." Jesus needed to be sure that the man had really thought carefully about what it would mean. "Foxes have holes," said Jesus, "and the birds of the air have nests, but the Son of Man has nowhere to lay his head."

Not long after this, Jesus chose seventy-two others – in addition to the twelve who were close to him – to help him with his work. He sent them on ahead, in pairs, to all the towns and villages he planned to visit himself, to prepare the people for his arrival.

"The harvest is rich," said Jesus, "but the labourers are few." He told his followers they should pray that God would call more people to help them with their mission. As he sent them on their way, he gave them clear instructions: "Remember I am sending you out like lambs among wolves. Carry no purse, no haversack, no sandals. Do not speak to anyone you pass on the road.

"When you stop at a house your first words should be 'Peace to this house!' and if good people live there your blessing will rest on them. Stay in that house and take whatever hospitality they offer you. When you visit a town where they make you welcome, cure those who are sick and tell them the kingdom of God is close to them, but if they do not make you welcome there, then wipe the dust of that town from your feet and leave.

"Anyone who listens to you, listens to me," said Jesus. "And those who reject you, reject me and my Father who sent me."

The ploughman

Jesus often used images of farming in his parables and stories. Ploughing the land was hard work. The wooden plough was drawn by oxen or asses. With one hand the farmer guided the plough and pressed it down, while the other hand held the stick, or goad, to drive the animals on. It was hot and tiring work, but it had to be done if the farmer hoped to harvest a good crop. The ploughman never looked back, but kept going until the work was finished.

One day, a man who had heard Jesus teaching was so moved by what Jesus had said that he came up to him afterwards. "Lord, I want to follow you and be your disciple!" he said, eagerly. "But just let me go back home and say goodbye to my family and friends."

Jesus shook his head. "Once the hand is laid on the plough," he said, "no one who looks back is fit for the kingdom of God."

Peter believes in Jesus

Jesus and his disciples crossed over the Sea of Galilee to the coast of Caesarea Philippi, on the other side, away from the crowds. There Jesus was able to teach them and warn them all to be on their guard against the strict Jews – the Pharisees and Sadducees – who would try and destroy their faith in him. Then he put this question to them: "Who do people say that I am?"

They thought about this for a while. "Some say you are John the Baptist," they said. "Others think you are Elijah, or Jeremiah, or one of the other prophets."

"But who do *you* think I am?" asked Jesus.

Simon Peter spoke up immediately. "You are Christ, the Messiah," he said. "Son of the living God."

Jesus said to Simon Peter, "You are happy and fortunate, because my Father in heaven himself has revealed this truth to you. And so I now tell *you* that you are Peter – a name that means rock – and it is upon you that I will build my church. It will stand firm and solid against the forces of evil. And you shall be given the keys of heaven, too."

Jesus rebukes Peter

Jesus ordered his disciples not to tell anyone that they knew he was the promised Messiah. He told them that he had to go to Jerusalem, where he would suffer and die at the hands of the Jewish leaders. But on the third day he would rise again from death.

The disciples were appalled. Like other faithful Jews at that time, they all thought that the Messiah was going to lead them all in to the glory of God's kingdom. What was all this talk of suffering and death?

Peter took Jesus to one side. "This must not happen to you, Lord!" he cried.

Jesus turned away sharply. "Get behind me, Satan!" he said. "You are trying to stop me from fulfilling my mission! You are thinking of yourself, not God."

Jesus came on Earth to be our Saviour: it was only by giving his life for us that he could accomplish this.

Jesus is transfigured

A week later, Jesus took his closest disciples – Peter, James and John – up Mount Hermon to pray.

While they were praying, the appearance of Jesus suddenly changed: his face shone like the sun and his clothes became brighter than the snow on the mountain. Two other figures appeared with Jesus: Moses and Elijah. Peter, James and John were terrified.

Then a cloud covered Jesus and a voice said, "This is my beloved Son. Listen to him."

The disciples fell to the ground, covering their faces. When they looked up again, they saw only Jesus. He walked down the mountain with them and warned them not to tell anyone what they had seen until after his resurrection. But they were too scared to ask him what he meant.

Martha and Mary

Continuing on his journey, Jesus came to the village of Bethany, outside Jerusalem. Here, he was welcomed by a woman called Martha, who invited him into the house she shared with her sister, Mary.

Having made her guest comfortable, Martha set to work, busily preparing a fine meal and bustling about serving refreshments.

All this while, Mary sat quietly at the feet of Jesus, listening attentively to everything he said.

Eventually, Martha became flustered with having to do everything herself and seeing her sister do nothing to help with the preparation of their meal.

"Lord," she said crossly, "doesn't it bother you that my sister is leaving me to do all the work by myself? Please tell her to help me."

"Martha, Martha," said Jesus, gently. "You worry and fret about so many things, when it's not necessary. It is much more important to listen to me while I am here with you, as Mary is doing, than to worry about housework."

Talking to God

From time to time Jesus left his disciples to go off by himself to pray. He knew how important it was to have quiet times alone with his heavenly Father.

One day his disciples said to Jesus, "Lord, how should we pray and talk to God?"

Jesus replied, "When you pray, say this:

Father, may your name always be held holy.
May your kingdom come.
Give us each day the bread we need,
And forgive our sins, just as we forgive others
    who have done wrong to us.
Do not put us to the test, but keep us safe from
    all evil."

The way to pray

Jesus said, "When you pray, tell God what you need. Be sure that he will answer your prayer, and don't be afraid to keep on asking.

"Just suppose a friend of yours arrives without warning in the middle of the night. He's tired and hungry, but you have no food in the house. So you go round to a neighbour to ask for help. 'Can you please lend me some bread?' you call. 'My friend's just arrived and I've nothing to give him to eat!'

"Your neighbour is probably going to be annoyed. 'Go away!' he says, 'it's the middle of the night and my family and I are trying to sleep!' But you don't go away. You keep on asking and knocking until your neighbour finally gives you everything you need, just to make you leave him in peace.

"This is how you should pray," said Jesus. "Don't give up. Ask, and God will give it to you. Look for him, and you will find him. Knock, and he will open the door to you himself, for he never turns anyone away."

Jesus and the woman at the well

One day Jesus was travelling through Samaria with his disciples, on his way to Galilee. At midday he rested by a well while his disciples went off to buy some food. A Samaritan woman came to the well to draw water and Jesus asked her for a drink.

"Why would a Jew ask a Samaritan for a drink?" she asked. The Jews had always hated the Samaritans.

Jesus replied, "If you knew who I am, you would ask me for a drink and I would give you living water. The water from this well will only quench your thirst, but the water I'm offering will give eternal life."

"Sir," said the woman, "although my people worship

God in their own way, I know that a Saviour is coming who will explain the truth to us."

"I am the Christ," said Jesus, "speaking to you now."

The woman hurried back to the town and told everyone she knew that she had met the Messiah. They ran to Jesus and begged him to stay. So he stayed for two days, and many Samaritans came to believe in him.

Beware of greed

When a Jewish man died, it was usual for his money to be shared between his children. If they argued about it, they could take the matter to a court of law where a judge would decide what was fair.

One day, a man in the crowd came up to Jesus and said to him, "Master, my father has died and my brother won't give me my share of our inheritance. Please ask my brother to give me my share."

"My friend," said Jesus, "you cannot ask me to judge how your father's money should be shared out." Then he turned to the crowd.

"This is an important lesson for you," he said. "You must beware of greed of any kind, for your life does not depend on what you own. This is the way of the world. The world judges a person on the value of their possessions, but your real wealth is what is contained in your heart.

"Beware of storing up worldly treasure for yourself instead of making yourself rich in the sight of God."

Leaven in the dough

In those days the women got up early each morning and began making the bread for the family. First the women ground the grain (usually barley) between two large millstones. They then mixed the flour with water and salt, kneading the mixture into a soft dough. They pressed the dough into flat, rounded shapes. Sometimes they added a small amount of yeast – or leaven – to the flour, to make the dough rise and so produce lighter bread. Unleavened bread remained flat.

Jesus used the image of bread-making in one of the stories he told to describe the kingdom of God. "It is like the yeast a woman mixed into the flour," he said, "so that it was thoroughly leavened. It only takes a tiny piece of yeast to change the whole lump of dough."

God's Spirit is like that leaven. His kingdom has come, his followers are few, but those whose hearts are given to God have power to change the whole world – just as a little leaven changes the whole of the dough.

The rich young man

A rich young man came up to Jesus and asked him, "Master, what must I do to be sure of eternal life?"

"If you want to be sure of eternal life," said Jesus, "you should keep the commandments: do not kill anyone, do not take someone else's wife, do not steal, do not tell lies, do not cheat. Honour your father and mother, and love others as you love yourself."

"I have kept all of these," said the young man. "What else should I do?"

Jesus looked at him steadily and then said, "If you want to be perfect, sell all your possessions and give the money to the poor. That way you will have treasure in heaven. Then come back and follow me."

The young man was saddened by these words. He was very wealthy, and he simply could not give up his riches even for the kingdom of God.

Jesus turned to his disciples. "How hard it is for the rich to enter the kingdom of God," he said.

When they heard this, the disciples were astonished. They asked Jesus, "Then who can be saved?"

"For God, all things are possible," Jesus told them.

Wedding guests

Jesus taught that it was better to be humble than to try to impress: "When someone invites you to a wedding feast, don't rush to sit in the best seat. A more important guest might come after you, and the host will have to come and ask you to move further down the table in order to give your seat to the other guest. Instead, make your way to the lowest seat of all. Then your host will come up and say, 'My friend, please move higher up the table.' In that way, everyone at the table will see how honoured you are!"

Jesus used this example to teach his listeners about seeing themselves as God sees them. Pride separates us from God, as well as from each other. "Those who are proud," said Jesus, "will find themselves put down in the sight of God. But those who are already humble will be raised up and exalted by God."

Guests for a feast

One of the guests listening to Jesus remarked how wonderful it would be to be invited to a feast in the kingdom of God!

Jesus then told him a story: "There was once a rich man who arranged a fine banquet for his friends and sent out a great many invitations. On the day of the feast he sent his servant to tell the guests that everything was ready and they should come at once. However, one by one they all started to make excuses.

"'I've just bought a field,' said one. 'I have to go and inspect it.'

"'I've just bought five yoke of oxen,' said another. 'I must go and examine them.'

"'I've just got married,' said another, 'and I can't leave my new wife on her own.'

"The servant went back to his master and told him everything they had said. The rich man was furious. 'Go out quickly into the town,' he told the servant. 'Search all the streets and alleys and bring back all the poor and homeless to my feast.'

"The servant hurried away and did as he was told. 'Sir,' he told his master, 'I have done as you asked, but there is still room for more.'

"'In that case,' said his master, 'go out into the country lanes and invite all the beggars you can find. I want my house filled with guests! None of the other people I invited to eat with me chose to come, so these others can enjoy themselves instead.'"

In this parable, the feast represents the kingdom of God. God sent out his prophets to his chosen people, telling them of his kingdom that was to come. Now Jesus invited them into the kingdom, but many of the Jews refused to listen or believe him. So God will offer his kingdom to others.

A foolish builder

Great crowds came to hear the stories Jesus told. They were eager to understand the way they should live their lives in order to enter the kingdom of God.

Jesus told them that it was not easy for people to give themselves completely to God. Greed, selfishness, ambition, worldly desires – even families – all got in the way at one time or another. It is important that we come prepared to give up all these things. Entering God's kingdom is costly, but the rewards are great.

"Consider all these things before you decide," said Jesus. "For instance, imagine you were a builder about to build a tower. You would first of all draw up the plans and work out all the costs. Otherwise, you might find that halfway through the project you haven't enough money to finish it. You'd have to abandon the work and people would laugh at you for being so foolish."

Anyone who wants to build a home for God in their heart must first of all work out if they can afford the cost and commitment.

"As another example," said Jesus, "what king would march to war against another king without first sitting down and considering whether his army was big enough to conquer the other king's army? If it wasn't, then the king would send his ambassadors to his enemy, to find peaceful ways to end the war. In the same way, none of you can be my disciple unless you give up all the things you love most."

Workers in the vineyard

Jesus said, "The kingdom of heaven is just like the owner of a vineyard, whose crop was ready for harvesting. At dawn, he hurried down to the market place to hire workers to help him pick the grapes.

"He found a number of men there, standing round with nothing to do. 'Come and work in my vineyard,' said the farmer, 'and I'll pay you one denarius.' This was a Roman silver coin. It was a good wage for a day's work. The men went off cheerfully to start harvesting the grapes in the vineyard.

"The farmer went out again later in the day – at nine o'clock, noon and three o'clock. He hired every man he could find. Finally he went out again at five o'clock, when there was only one hour of the working day left, and found yet more men in the market place.

"'Why are you hanging around here with nothing to do?' asked the farmer.

"'No one wants to hire us,' said the men.

"'Well, you can go and help in my vineyard as well,' said the farmer. 'You can put in an hour of work for me.'

"Well pleased, the men joined all the others picking the farmer's grapes."

Paying the workers

Jesus continued the story, saying, "That evening, when the work ended at last, the farmer gave his bailiff a bag of money. 'Give everyone a full day's pay,' he said, 'starting with the men I took on last of all.'

"The men who had been at work since dawn expected to get more than all the others. They were extremely angry when the bailiff only gave them one denarius.

"'We've been working all day in the hot sun!' they cried. 'Yet you've paid us the same as these people who've only worked for an hour!'

"'My friends,' said the farmer, when he heard their complaints, 'I am not being unfair. We agreed, didn't we, that you would work for one denarius? Take your wages and go. If I decide I want to pay everyone the same amount, it is not your place to complain. Why be envious if I am generous?'"

"Those who arrive last are equal to those who arrive first," said Jesus, meaning that God's love is the same for everyone, and all those who enter the kingdom of God receive the same generous reward of eternal life.

Jesus feeds a crowd

A very large crowd of over five thousand people gathered by the Sea of Galilee to be with Jesus. They had heard of the wonderful things he had done and wanted to see him for themselves. Jesus climbed a hillside with his disciples and looked down on them all. Then he turned to Philip.

"Where can we buy some bread for these people to eat?" he asked him. It was a test: Jesus knew just what he was going to do.

Philip was appalled. "It would cost a fortune to feed them all!" he said.

"There's a young lad here," said Andrew, "with five barley loaves and two fishes. But that won't go very far amongst all these people!"

"Tell everyone to sit down," said Jesus.

When they were settled, Jesus took the five loaves, gave thanks to God, and blessed them. He handed them to his disciples to share out amongst the people. Then he did the same with the fish.

Everyone ate as much as they wanted, and when the leftovers were collected, they filled twelve baskets.

When the people saw this wonderful sign of his power they knew that Jesus had truly come from God. This was indeed the Saviour they had all been promised!

Jesus saw that they were about to force him to become their king, so he slipped away from them unnoticed and escaped into the hills by himself.

The unjust judge

Jesus told this story to his disciples to teach them not to lose heart when praying.

"There was a judge who cared little about poor people and had no fear of God. He was more interested in the bribes he could take from the rich. A poor widow needed his help in obtaining justice against a rogue who was cheating her, but she had no money to bribe this judge.

"The judge refused to listen to her, but the widow was determined. Every morning she was at his court, pleading for justice. She gave the judge no peace, night or day.

"Eventually the judge could stand it no longer. 'This widow is worrying me to death,' he said. 'There's only one way to put an end to her pestering, and that's to give her what she wants.'

"Even this hard-hearted judge gave the widow what she needed," said Jesus. "How much more readily will your heavenly Father, who loves all his children, answer you when you cry to him night and day, even though he may take time to answer."

Zacchaeus the tax collector

Jesus went through the town of Jericho on his way to Jerusalem. The chief tax collector there was a man called Zacchaeus. He had heard a great deal about Jesus and was keen to see him. But Zacchaeus was rather short and it was difficult for him to push his way through the crowds that always surrounded Jesus.

Then Zacchaeus had an idea. He ran on ahead and climbed up into a sycamore tree at the side of the road. From there he had a good view.

But as Jesus passed beneath the tree, he stopped and looked up. "Zacchaeus, come down from there," he called. "I'd like to come and stay at your house today!"

Zacchaeus was overjoyed, and couldn't climb down fast enough.

But as he and Jesus made their way to his house, Zacchaeus heard some of the people in the crowd grumbling. "It's not right for a man of God to go into the house of a sinful tax collector!" they said. Of all the people that worked for the Romans, tax collectors were the most hated because when they collected taxes for the Romans they made a great deal of money for themselves at the same time.

Immediately Zacchaeus turned to Jesus. "Look, Lord," he said. "I am going to give half my money to the poor. And if I've cheated anyone, I'll pay them back four times what I owe them!"

"Today, salvation has come to this house," said Jesus, for everyone to hear. "For I have come to seek out and to save that which was lost."

The last supper

It was time for Jesus to be glorified as the Son of God. He sent Peter and John into the city of Jerusalem to make preparations for them all to eat the Passover supper together.

"Where do you want us to meet?" they asked him.

"When you get to the city you will see a man carrying a jug of water. Follow him into the house he enters and say to the owner of the house, 'The Master asks: Where is the dining-room where I can eat the Passover meal with my disciples?' He'll show you a large room upstairs furnished just how we need it. That's where you are to prepare the meal."

Later, when they had all taken their places at the

supper table, Jesus told them just how special this meal was going to be. "I shall not eat another meal with you," he said, "or drink wine again until everything has been fulfilled." Then he took some of the bread, gave thanks and blessed it. He broke the bread and handed it to his disciples, saying, "Take this and eat: this is my body, which will be given for you."

Then Jesus lifted up his cup of wine, blessed it and passed it round, saying, "This cup is the new covenant in my blood, which will be shed for you. Do this to remember me."

For two thousand years since, Christians have remembered Jesus in the sharing of bread and wine in the Eucharist, or Holy Communion.

Jesus washes the feet of the disciples

In those days, it was the custom for the host at a meal to have a servant ready to wash the hot and dusty feet of his guests.

While the disciples were seated at the supper table, Jesus stood up, took off his outer garment and wrapped a towel round his waist. Then he poured water into a basin and began to wash the feet of each of his disciples.

When he reached Peter, however, Peter was horrified. "Lord, are you going to wash my feet?" he asked him.

"At the moment you don't understand what I am doing," Jesus told him, "but it will become clear soon."

"Never!" said Peter. "You shall never wash my feet!" Peter was shocked. It was unthinkable that Jesus should perform such a lowly task.

"If you do not let me wash your feet," said Jesus, "you cannot belong to me."

Then Peter understood. "Then, Lord, don't just wash my feet – wash all of me!"

"No, you are already clean," said Jesus. Then he looked around the table. "But not all of you are." He knew one of them had evil in his heart and would soon betray him.

"I have given you all an example to follow," he said. "If I, your Lord and Master, have washed your feet like any ordinary servant, then you too should be servants of each other and be prepared to wash each other's feet."

Judas plots to betray Jesus

Of all his disciples, Judas Iscariot alone did not approve of some of the things Jesus did. Judas looked after their common fund, which was used to pay for their simple needs and help the poor, and he was known to have helped himself on occasion. It was easy for Satan to enter his heart.

Judas had secretly gone to see the members of the Jewish council: the Sanhedrin. He knew they wanted to arrest Jesus, and they discussed how he might help.

Judas agreed to their offer of thirty pieces of silver, and the deal was struck.

During the last supper, Jesus announced that one of them would betray him. John, sitting beside Jesus, leaned over and asked him quietly, "Who is it, Lord?"

"The one to whom I shall give this piece of bread," said Jesus. He handed it to Judas, saying, "Do what you have to do quickly!" The other disciples did not know what he meant, but thought Jesus was telling Judas to give some of their funds to the poor.

As soon as Judas had taken the bread, he slipped away into the night.

In the garden of Gethsemane

After supper, Jesus led his disciples to a quiet garden called Gethsemane, on the Mount of Olives. Telling the others to wait for him, he went inside to pray with Peter, James and John.

"Keep watch while I pray," he said, and went a little way to be alone with his heavenly Father. He threw himself to the ground in agony, for he knew what terrible things were in store for him. "Father," he prayed, "all things are possible to you. If it is your will, take this cup of suffering away from me."

After a while, Jesus came back to his disciples and found them fast asleep. "Could you not watch with me for one hour?" he asked. They were ashamed, but when Jesus went away again they still could not stay awake. Twice more Jesus returned and found them asleep.

"Are you still sleeping?" Jesus asked them when he returned the third time. "It is time to wake up: my hour is here. Now I shall be betrayed into the hands of evil men. Get up! My betrayer is already on his way."

Judas betrays Jesus

Judas knew where Jesus would be. He had often visited Gethsemane with Jesus and the other disciples. This time, Judas came into the garden with a number of men carrying clubs and swords, sent by the Sanhedrin.

Judas had arranged a signal with them: "The man I go up to and kiss," he said, "is the one you want. Take him into custody and make sure you have him well-guarded when you lead him away in case any of his friends try to rescue him."

He then went boldly up to Jesus and kissed him on the cheek. "Master!" he said.

"My friend," said Jesus, sadly. "Would you betray me with a kiss?"

The men seized Jesus. But just then Simon Peter drew his sword and struck the high priest's servant, cutting off his ear.

"Put away your sword," said Jesus. "Those who live by the sword will die by the sword. This is the way it must be!" He touched the man's ear and immediately it was healed.

Then Jesus turned to his captors. "Am I such a criminal," he asked, "that you need to take me with swords and clubs? I was with you all in the temple day after day. Why didn't you arrest me then?"

They said nothing, but tied Jesus' hands and led him away to the high priest.

Afraid for their lives, his followers all ran and left him. The armed men caught hold of one young man. He was wearing nothing but a linen tunic, which he shrugged off and ran away naked rather than be arrested.

Judas is sorry

Early next morning, the chief priests and elders of the people decided that Jesus should be put to death.

We will never really know why Judas betrayed Jesus. It may be that since he loved money so much, he wanted Jesus to become a powerful king on earth, so that Judas could be powerful, too, as his treasurer.

Whatever his reasons, it is clear that Judas had not intended that Jesus should be condemned to death. As soon as he heard that Jesus was to die, Judas was filled with remorse.

He went straight to the Sanhedrin with the thirty pieces of silver he had been given.

"I have made a terrible mistake," Judas told them. "I have betrayed an innocent man."

"Why should we worry?" said the chief priests. "That's your problem, not ours."

Appalled, Judas threw the money down in the sanctuary of the temple, and ran out. Unable to bear the enormity of what he had done, Judas hanged himself.

The chief priests picked up the coins from the temple floor and wondered what they should do with them.

"It's against the law for it to be put into the temple treasury," they said. "It's blood-money."

In the end, they decided to use the money to buy a potter's field, to turn it into a graveyard for foreigners. And even to this day, Jerusalem's cemetery for foreigners is known as the Field of Blood.

Peter breaks his promise

Peter had been horrified at the things that had happened in the Garden of Gethsemane. He had tried to save Jesus from his attackers, drawing his sword and slashing off the ear of a man called Malchus, the high priest's servant. But then Jesus had commanded him to put his sword away and had healed the injured man.

Helpless, Peter could only stand in the shadows and watch while the men bound the master he loved and led him away. He and John followed at a distance, and saw them take Jesus into the palace of Annas, the high priest.

Now John was acquainted with the high priest, so leaving Peter outside, he went in and spoke to the woman on duty at the door, asking her if they could both come inside. As soon as the maid saw Peter she said, "Aren't you another of that man's disciples?"

"No, I'm not!" said Peter, quickly. He went over to the fireside, where the servants and guards were warming themselves.

"Here, you were with him too, weren't you?" asked one of them.

"No, my friend," said Peter. "You are mistaken."

Then another servant – a relative of Malchus, in fact – said, "Didn't I see you in the garden with him?"

"No – I don't know what you're talking about!" shouted Peter.

Just then a cock crowed and Peter remembered that Jesus had said: "Before the cock crows you will deny me three times."

He had promised Jesus, "Even if I have to die, I will never deny you!"

Peter ran outside, threw himself on the ground and wept bitterly.

Jesus before King Herod

Although the Jewish leaders had tried Jesus and found him guilty, they had to ask Pilate, the Roman governor, to pass the death sentence. Only the governor could order an execution.

They brought Jesus before Pilate.

Pilate questioned Jesus himself. "Have you heard all the charges the council have brought against you?" he asked. "How do you answer them?"

But Jesus said nothing.

"I find no case against this man," Pilate told the council.

However, the Jewish leaders persisted, so determined were they to get rid of Jesus. "He has stirred up the people throughout the land with his teaching, from Galilee all the way here to Jerusalem!" they said.

When Pilate heard the name Galilee, he asked if Jesus came from there. As this was the case, he came under the responsibility of King Herod, the ruler of Galilee. And it so happened that Herod was staying in Jerusalem at that time, so Pilate sent Jesus to him.

Herod was delighted. He had heard all about Jesus and the miracles he had performed, and had wanted to meet him. He was hoping that Jesus could work some marvel for him to see.

King Herod asked Jesus many questions, but all the time he was questioned, Jesus remained silent. Then the chief priests angrily threw accusations at him.

Finally, tired of trying to make Jesus answer him, Herod and his guards dressed Jesus up as a king in a splendid robe and made fun of him. Then Herod sent Jesus back to Pilate so that the governor could decide what to do with him.

After many years of being enemies, Herod and Pilate now became friends.

Jesus before the Roman governor

Pilate summoned the chief priests. "You have brought this man, Jesus, before me, accused of crimes against the state," he told them. "Well, I have found no case against him. Neither has Herod: he has sent him back to us. This man has done nothing to deserve death, so I shall have him flogged and then released."

The Jewish leaders were furious. "We want him crucified!" they shouted.

Pilate did not want to cause a riot, but he couldn't just hand over an innocent man to be executed. So he ordered Jesus to be brought before him for questioning again. "Are you really the king of the Jews?" he asked him.

"Is this your own question," said Jesus, "or are you just repeating what others have said?"

"Am I a Jew?" snapped Pilate. "It's your own people and the chief priests who have handed you over to me. What have you done?"

"My kingdom is not of this world," replied Jesus. "If it was, my followers would have fought to save me from my enemies."

"You are a king, then?" said Pilate.

"Yes, I am a king. I was born to bring truth into the world. All those on the side of truth listen to my voice."

"Truth?" said Pilate, crossly. "What is that?" And he went back out to face the crowds.

Barabbas the robber

It was the custom at the Passover festival for the governor to release a prisoner for the people – anyone they chose. There was a man in prison at that time called Barabbas, who had caused a riot and committed murder. So, when the people came to ask Pilate for the release of a prisoner, Pilate asked them, "Do you want me to release the king of the Jews?" He knew very well that the chief priests were jealous of Jesus and that was why they wanted to get rid of him.

At that moment, Pilate received a message from his wife. She warned her husband not to have anything to do with Jesus of Nazareth. "He is innocent. I have been upset all day by a dream I had about him," she said.

"No," replied the people to Pilate's question. "We want Barabbas." The chief priests had already told them what to say.

"What shall I do with the man you call the king of the Jews?" Pilate asked them.

"Crucify him! Crucify him!"

"But what harm has he done?" said Pilate.

But the people just shouted, "We want Barabbas!"

Pilate could see that they were becoming dangerous. So he sent for a bowl of water, and in front of the crowds he washed his hands. "I am innocent of this man's blood," he told them.

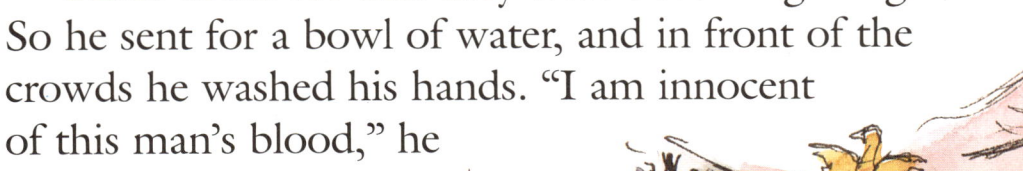

"His blood be on us and on our children!" shouted the people.

Pilate gives in

Pilate had Jesus taken away and flogged. Afterwards, the soldiers twisted some thorns into a crown and put it on his head, and dressed him in a purple robe. They kept coming up to him saying, "Hail! King of the Jews!" and slapping him round the face.

Once more, Pilate went out to speak to the crowd. He had Jesus led out with him, still wearing the crown of thorns and purple robe. "Here is the man," said Pilate. "I find no case against him."

But the crowd shouted, "Crucify him! Crucify him!"

"Take him yourselves and crucify him," said Pilate, "for I find him innocent."

"We have a law," replied the Jews, "and according to the law he ought to die because he claimed to be the Son of God."

Pilate became even more anxious to set Jesus free.

"If you free him," said the Jews, "you are no friend of Caesar. Anyone who makes himself a king is defying the Emperor!"

When he heard these words, Pilate took his place in the Judgement Seat. "Here is your king," he said to the Jews. "Do you want me to crucify him?"

"We have no king except Caesar!" they replied.

So Pilate handed Jesus over to be crucified.

Jesus dies on the cross

Jesus was taken outside the city of Jerusalem to a place called Golgotha, or Skull Hill. There, he was nailed to the cross and the soldiers set it upright in the ground. Two thieves were crucified with Jesus, one on either side of him. Jesus prayed: "Father, forgive them. They do not know what they do."

A notice was fixed on the cross above Jesus' head, on the orders of Pontius Pilate, which read: *Jesus of Nazareth, King of the Jews* in Hebrew, Greek and Latin.

Four women stayed by the cross with Jesus. One of them was his mother, Mary. Beside her stood John, the disciple who had been closest to Jesus. Jesus said to his mother, "This is your son, now," and to John he said, "This is your mother." And from that moment, John took Mary into his home and looked after her.

The Jewish leaders wanted the bodies of Jesus and the two thieves to be removed before sunset, when the Sabbath began. The soldiers broke the legs of the thieves to make sure they were dead, but Jesus was already dead, so one soldier pierced his side with a lance instead, and immediately blood and water ran down.

Everything happened just as scripture had said it would.

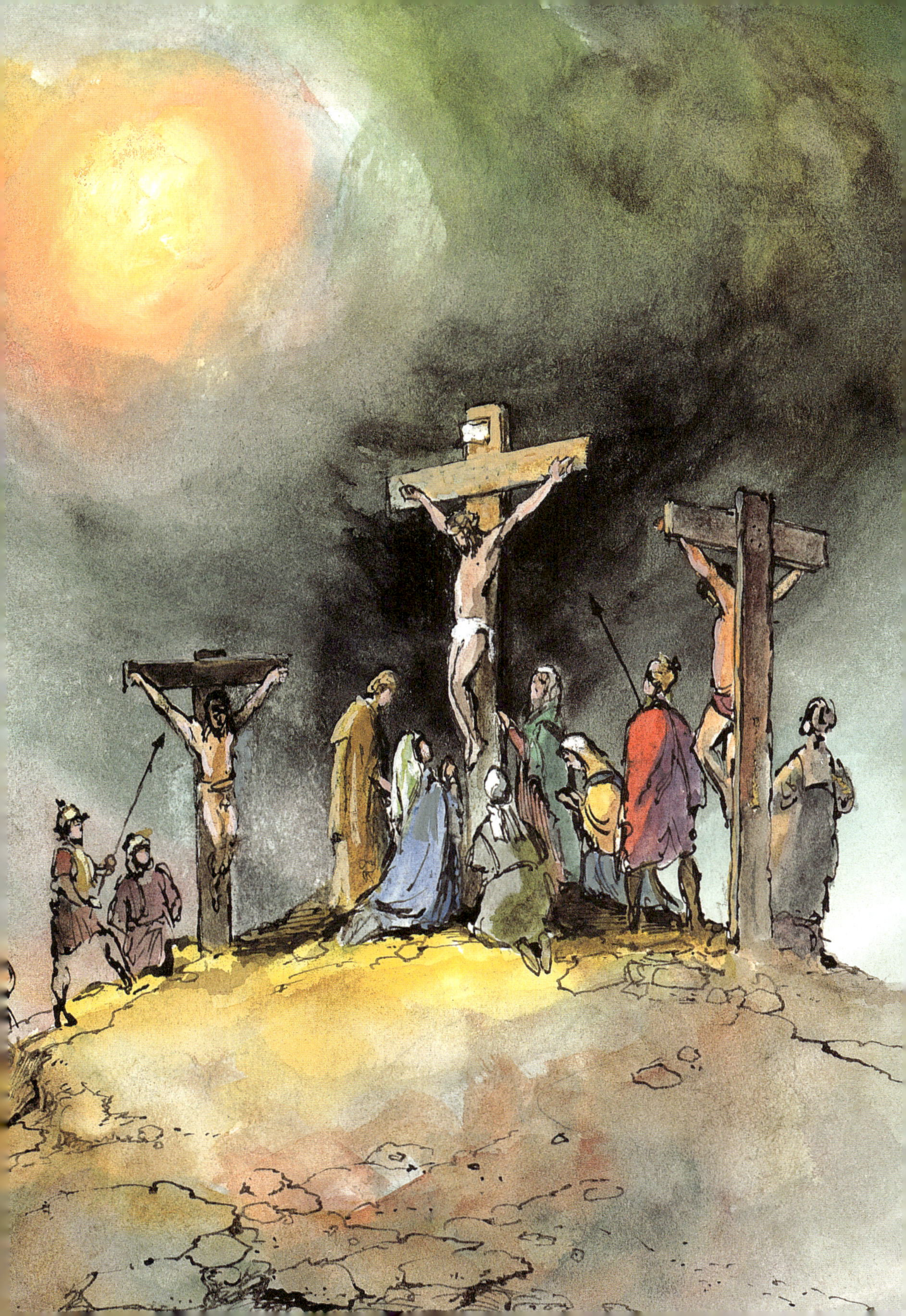

Jesus is taken down from the cross

One of the secret followers of Jesus was a rich man called Joseph, who came from a hill town called Arimathea. Joseph went to Pilate and asked if he could take the body of Jesus and bury it.

Pilate was surprised that Jesus should have died so soon. He called for his centurion to confirm that this was the case, and then he gave his permission for the body to be removed. Joseph and his friend Nicodemus – another secret disciple – took the body of Jesus down from the cross, wrapped it in a clean shroud, and carried it to a place not far from Golgotha where Joseph had a newly-built tomb intended for his own family. They laid the body of Jesus in the tomb.

Nicodemus had brought with him a special mixture of myrrh and aloes, weighing about a hundred pounds. They anointed the body of Jesus with these spices, then they wrapped it in clean linen cloths, following the usual custom for a Jewish burial.

When the body had been laid carefully on the stone ledge inside the cave, Joseph and Nicodemus rolled a great stone across its entrance, to make it secure.

Outside, Mary Magdalene and the other women watched and waited, taking note of where Jesus was buried. They would have to wait until after the Sabbath before they could come and anoint the body of Jesus themselves.

Meanwhile, the Jewish leaders went to see Pilate again. "Your Excellency," they said. "If you remember, this man pretending to be the Messiah made a promise before he died, that in three days he would rise from death. We suggest, then, that you give the order for the tomb to be made secure and a guard put in front of it until the third day, to make sure that his followers do not try to steal the body and make out that Jesus has risen! This fraud would be worse than all the others!"

"You may have your guard," said Pilate. "Make the tomb as secure as you know how."

So the chief priests put seals on the stone outside the tomb and soldiers took turns to guard it day and night.

The empty tomb

Very early on the morning after the Sabbath, Mary Magdalene came to the tomb with a friend. The two women had been wondering whom they could ask to roll the stone away for them, but they were astonished to see that it had already been removed. Going inside the tomb, they saw that the body of Jesus had gone.

For a moment they did not know what to do.

Just then, two angels in brilliant clothes appeared beside them. The women were terrified and fell to the ground.

"Do not be afraid," said the angels. "Why are you looking among the dead for someone who has risen?

Remember what Jesus told you: that the son of Man had to be handed over to be crucified, but that on the third day he would rise again."

The women remembered, and immediately hurried away to tell Peter and the other disciples what they had seen.

When the apostles heard the women's account, they did not believe them. But Peter and John ran to the tomb to see for themselves.

John arrived first and stopped at the open doorway. He could see it was empty. Then Peter came and went right inside.

The disciples saw the linen cloths on the ground, and also the cloth that had covered the head of Jesus, rolled up neatly on the stone ledge.

Until this moment, they had not understood what Jesus had told them, but now they believed that he had indeed risen from the dead!

Doubting Thomas

In the evening of that same day, the disciples were together in the upper room, hiding from the Jews. Although the door was securely locked, Jesus came and stood among them. "Peace be with you," he said, and he showed them the marks in his hands and in his side.

Now Thomas, one of the twelve, was not with the others at this time. When they told him the wonderful things that had happened, and how Jesus had just been with them, Thomas could not believe that it was all true.

"Unless I see him for myself and can touch the wounds in his hands and side," he said, "I refuse to believe."

Eight days later the disciples were in the house again, this time with Thomas. The doors were locked as before. Suddenly, Jesus was there among them.

"Peace be with you," he said, and turned to Thomas. "Here are my hands, Thomas. Look, here is the wound in my side. Doubt no longer, but believe!"

Thomas fell to his knees in front of Jesus. "My Lord and my God!" he cried.

"You believe because you can see me," said Jesus. "How happy are those who have not seen me and yet believe in me."

117

The road to Emmaus

That same day, two disciples were on their way home from Jerusalem to a village called Emmaus. As they walked, talking over the terrible things that had happened in the last few days, Jesus himself came up and walked beside them. But something prevented the two men from recognising him.

"What are you discussing that makes you so sad?" Jesus asked them.

"Haven't you heard?" they replied. "Jesus of Nazareth, the one we believed was the promised Messiah, has been put to death."

Jesus shook his head. "Why are you so slow to believe everything the prophets told you would happen? Didn't they say that the Messiah should suffer and then be glorified?" And beginning with Moses and the prophets he explained to them all the passages in scripture that referred to himself.

When they reached Emmaus, the two disciples invited Jesus to have supper with them. When they sat down to eat, Jesus took up the bread, blessed it and gave it to them. And at that moment, the disciples recognised him. Jesus, however, disappeared.

Immediately the two friends returned to Jerusalem to tell the other disciples their wonderful news.

Jesus appears for the third time

Peter, James and John and four other disciples went out fishing one night, but they returned to the shore empty-handed.

A man was waiting for them on the shore. He called out as they brought in the boat: "Have you caught anything?"

"No," they shouted back.

"Throw out the net to starboard and you'll catch some fish," said the stranger.

So they dropped the net into the water again and immediately it became so full of fish that they could not pull it back in.

"It is the Lord!" said John. Peter looked across at the man on the shore, then he grabbed his cloak and leaped into the water to join Jesus, leaving the others to bring in the catch.

When the others came ashore, Jesus had breakfast ready for them: bread and some fish cooking on a charcoal fire. After they had eaten, Jesus turned to Peter.

"Simon Peter," he said, "do you love me more than these others do?"

Peter answered, "Lord, you know I do."

"Feed my lambs," said Jesus. Then he asked Peter again, "Simon Peter, do you love me?"

Peter said, "Yes, Lord, you know I love you."

Then Jesus asked a third time, "Simon Peter, do you love me?"

Peter was upset that Jesus should ask him three times. "Lord, you know everything; you know I love you!"

Jesus said to him, "Feed my sheep."

Then Peter understood, and the shame of his earlier denial of Jesus was lifted from him.

The Ascension

For forty days after the Passion, Jesus continued to appear to the apostles on many occasions. Then one day he took them out as far as Bethany, instructing them not to leave Jerusalem just yet. "Wait for what my Father has promised," he told them. "As I told you before, John baptised with water, but in a few days time you will be baptised with the Holy Spirit."

But they were still slow to understand. Now that he had returned to them, the disciples still thought that one day Jesus would triumphantly establish the kingdom for which they all longed.

"Lord," they asked him, "has the time come for you to restore the kingdom to Israel?"

Jesus told them that his heavenly Father would decide these things. In the meantime, they had an extraordinary mission to undertake. "You will receive the power of the Holy Spirit when I am gone," he said. "Then you will be my witnesses not only in Jerusalem but throughout Judaea, Samaria and, in fact, right to the ends of the earth!"

Then he raised his hands to bless them. And suddenly, while they watched, he was lifted up and a cloud took him out of sight.

They were still staring upwards, long after he had gone, when two men in white were suddenly standing beside them.

"Why are you men from Galilee all looking up into

the sky?" they asked the disciples. "Jesus has been taken up into heaven. One day he will return in the same way as you have seen him go."

The disciples praised God and went back to Jerusalem with their hearts full of joy.

Peter the leader

The disciples went back to Jerusalem, to the upper room where they had been staying since they shared the Passover supper together, to await the Holy Spirit. They were Peter, John, James, Andrew, Philip, Thomas, Bartholomew and Matthew, James (the son of Alphaeus), Simon the Zealot and Jude. It was dangerous for them to be seen in the city, as the Jews were arresting anyone they suspected of being a follower of Jesus.

At that time, several faithful women joined them, including Mary the mother of Jesus, and they all prayed together continuously. Altogether there were about one hundred and twenty followers of Jesus in Jerusalem at that time.

One day, Peter stood up and spoke to them all. Jesus had chosen him to care for his church, and from once having been a fearful, simple fisherman, Peter now showed himself to be a strong leader. Their first task, he told the others, was to appoint a disciple to take the place of the traitor, Judas Iscariot. They needed to choose someone who had been with them right from the time when John the Baptist had preached in the desert.

There were two candidates put forward: Joseph Barsabbas and Matthias. The disciples prayed, opening their hearts to God to guide their choice. Then they drew lots and Matthias was chosen to be the twelfth disciple.

125

Pentecost

Fifty days after Passover was the Jewish festival of Pentecost. As the disciples were praying together in the upper room, the sound of a powerful wind filled the entire house. Flames of fire hovered over each of their heads and they were all filled with the Holy Spirit.

Immediately they began to speak in foreign languages as the Spirit gave them the gift of speech and courage to praise God and proclaim the Good News of Jesus.

Peter proclaims the Good News

They rushed down into the temple square, where everyone was gathered for the festival, and began to preach. There were people from many different regions, from as far away as Egypt and Rome. Yet they all heard the disciples and were able to understand what they were saying.

Peter addressed the crowd in a loud voice: "Men of Israel! People of Judaea! We are not drunk, but have been filled by God's Holy Spirit. Listen to me! Jesus of Nazareth was sent by God, as his miracles proved. You killed him, but God raised him to life, freeing him from death. All of us have seen him and are witnesses to that. Now he has been raised to God's right hand, in heaven: the promised Saviour whom you crucified!"

The crowds were very upset at Peter's words. "What should we do?" they asked.

"You must be sorry for the things you have done wrong," said Peter, "and be baptised – every one of you – in the name of Jesus. Then you, too, will receive the gift of the Holy Spirit. This is God's promise to you and your children!"

That day about three thousand came to believe in the Good News and were baptised.

The lame man is cured

One afternoon as Peter and John went up to the temple together to pray, a crippled man was carried past them on a stretcher. He had never been able to walk. Every day his friends brought him to the temple gate so he could beg for money. He held out his hands to Peter and John as they walked by.

"Look at us!" said the disciples. The man looked up hopefully.

"I don't have money to give you," said Peter, "but I will give you what I can. In the name of Jesus of Nazareth, get up and walk!"

Peter took the man by the hand and helped him to stand. Instantly the man's legs and ankles became strong and he jumped around in delight, praising God.

Soon a large crowd gathered to see this astonishing sight. They were all familiar with the beggar who had sat day after day at the temple gate. Peter told them all the Good News of Jesus in whose name the man had been healed.

Peter and John are arrested

The priests of the temple were very angry that Peter and John should be preaching about Jesus and had them both arrested. They were brought before the council and high priest, Annas, the very next day. The two disciples stood in the middle of the court while the council asked them a great many questions.

Peter was filled with the Holy Spirit. "Rulers of the people and elders," he said. "If you are asking us today about an act of kindness to someone who was crippled, I am glad to tell you that it was by the name of Jesus Christ – the one you crucified – that this man is able to stand up, completely healed, in your presence."

The chief priests were astonished at how calm and assured these two men were. But while the man they had cured stood next to them, they could do nothing more than warn them not to preach again. They could not risk upsetting the crowds who had all seen what had happened. But Peter and the other apostles continued to teach at the gate of the temple every day, and heal the sick that were brought to them.

The apostles on trial

The angry temple priests had Peter and the apostles thrown into prison. But that same night an angel of the Lord freed them, and at dawn they returned to the temple. Astonished, the priests brought them before the Sanhedrin. "You were warned not to preach in the name of this Jesus," the high priest told them, "yet you go on doing so!"

Peter replied, "Obedience to God is more important than obedience to men. God has raised Jesus to be our Saviour. We are his witnesses."

The priests were furious. Many wanted the apostles to be put to death. But one of the elders, a wise man called Gamaliel, advised the council to wait.

If the apostles had indeed been sent by God, then God would protect them. If not, then they and their cause would simply disappear in time.

So the council had the apostles beaten and then set them free, with another warning not to preach any more. The apostles left, rejoicing that they had suffered for the name of Jesus, and went on telling everyone the Good News.

The stoning of Stephen

As the early church grew, the disciples needed help with day-to-day matters such as sharing out food and looking after the poor. Seven men were chosen for this work, one of them a young man called Stephen, who was already filled with the Holy Spirit. He began to work many miracles, so that people came from far and wide to see him.

One day, several Jewish priests came to listen to Stephen and debate the law with him. They wanted to catch him out, but the Holy Spirit gave Stephen answers for them. So they took Stephen to the Sanhedrin, accused of declaring the Jewish law old-fashioned.

The council members looked at Stephen and it seemed to them that his face shone like that of an angel.

"Is it true what these priests have said?" the high priest asked him.

"The chosen people have always misunderstood the prophets sent by God," Stephen told them. "You have tried to confine God to a building made by human hands, and resisted the Holy Spirit." The angry council members had Stephen taken away and stoned.

As he was dying, Stephen prayed: "Lord Jesus, receive my spirit. Do not hold this sin against them."

One of the crowd watching was a young man called Saul. Determined to destroy the church, Saul went from house to house arresting anyone suspected of following Jesus, and sending them to prison.

Philip and the Ethiopian

Another of the seven helpers was Philip. He escaped from Jerusalem and went into the towns and villages of Samaria to teach the people there about Jesus. He worked many miracles, too.

One day, the Holy Spirit instructed Philip to take the desert road that ran from Jerusalem to Gaza. Philip did so, and after a while he met a richly-dressed Ethiopian official from the court of the Queen of Egypt. He was, in fact, her chief treasurer, and was returning from a pilgrimage to Jerusalem with his servants.

As he approached, Philip heard the Ethiopian reading aloud from a scroll of the prophet Isaiah.

"Do you understand what you are reading?" Philip asked him.

"How can I," replied the Ethiopian, "unless someone helps me?" He invited Philip to sit in his chariot with him. Starting with the passage from Isaiah, Philip explained the Good News of Jesus to the Ethiopian.

They came to a place along the road where there was a pool of water.

"Would you please baptise me in this pool?" the Ethiopian asked Philip. They both got down from the chariot and Philip baptised him. But just as he came up out of the water, the Holy Spirit took Philip to another place where he was needed. The Ethiopian never saw Philip again, but he continued his journey home full of joy.

Saul on the road to Damascus

Saul came from a very religious Jewish family, and as a young man he went to study the sacred law at Jerusalem. Such was his zeal for the old Jewish law that he tirelessly hunted down and persecuted all the followers of Jesus. He even asked the high priest in Jerusalem to give him permission to extend his hunt to Damascus, and to bring prisoners back to Jerusalem for trial.

Before he reached the city of Damascus, however, something happened to change his life for ever. A great light from heaven suddenly shone all around Saul, so that he fell to the ground, terrified. Then a voice said, "Saul, Saul. Why are you persecuting me?"

"Who are you, Lord?" asked the trembling Saul.

"I am Jesus, and you are persecuting me," said the voice. "Get up now and go into the city, and you will be told what you have to do."

The men travelling with Saul were astonished. They saw the bright light, but they did not hear the voice. And when Saul stood up, he could not see a thing. His friends had to lead him into the city.

For three days Saul lay blind and unable to eat or drink, praying and waiting to hear what was to become of him.

Saul becomes a Christian

In the city of Damascus there lived a disciple called Ananias. He had a vision of Jesus in which the Lord said to him, "Go to Straight Street and ask at the house of Judas for someone called Saul who comes from Tarsus. At the moment he is praying. He has had a vision of a man called Ananias coming in and laying hands on him to give him back his sight."

Ananias was horrified. "Lord, I have heard of this man," he said. "People have told me of all the harm he has been doing to your faithful people in Jerusalem. He has come here with a warrant to arrest everyone who believes in you."

But the Lord said, "Go and see him anyway. I have chosen this man to bring my name before people of all nations, not just Jews. And I will show him just how much he will have to suffer for me."

So Ananias went as he was told and laid his hands on Saul, saying, "Brother Saul, the Lord Jesus who appeared to you on the road has sent me to you so that you may recover your sight and be filled with the Holy Spirit."

At once Saul was able to see again. Ananias baptised him there and then, and after taking some food and drink, Saul began to recover.

After his conversion, Saul spent a few days with the disciples in Damascus. He took the Roman form of his name – Paul – and began preaching the Good News of Jesus.

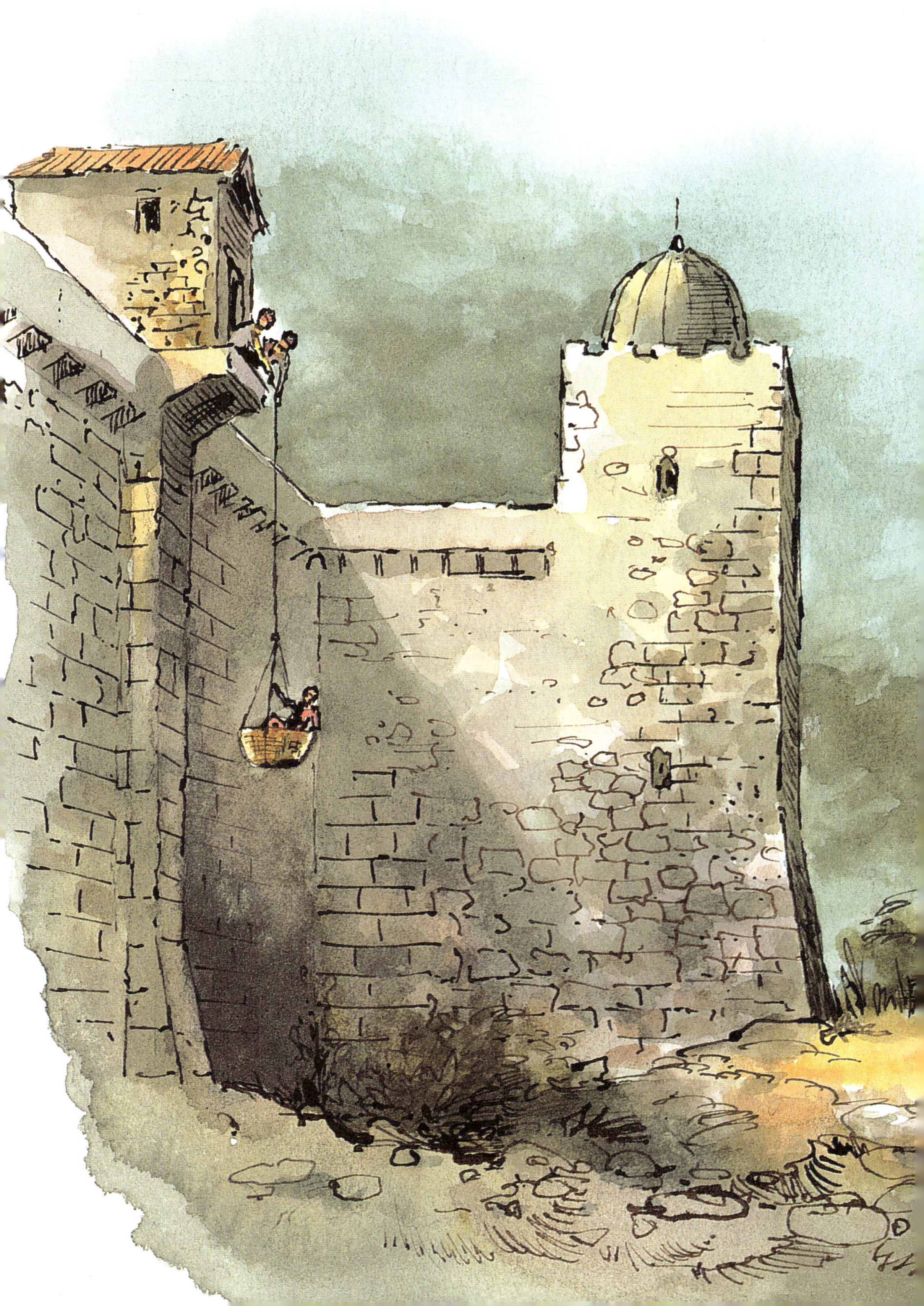

Paul begins his ministry

When Paul began preaching about Jesus, the Son of God, everyone who heard him was amazed. "Isn't this the man who came here to Damascus from Jerusalem to lead the attack on the followers of Christ?" they said.

Paul's power grew stronger and stronger. He completely confused the Jewish community, because they knew he was a very strict Jew, but now he was telling them to believe in the risen Christ, the Messiah. Gradually more Jews became followers of Jesus.

The Jewish leaders were furious with Paul and plotted to kill him. When it was dark, they lay in wait for him, guarding the gates to the city so he could not escape. But Paul's friends among the faithful heard of their plan. They helped Paul climb over the city wall and lowered him in a basket to safety.

Paul returned to Jerusalem. At first the Christians there were still afraid of him. Then one of the disciples, Barnabas, befriended Paul and took him to meet the apostles. Because his life was in danger, the brothers took Paul to Caesarea and from there he set off for Tarsus.

Peter at Jaffa

Peter, meanwhile, visited one place after another, spreading the Good News as well.

In the coastal town of Jaffa there was a woman called Tabitha (also known by her Greek name, Dorcas) who was a very faithful Christian. She was always doing good and giving to the poor, and was well known for her skilful needlework.

There was great sorrow among the Christian community when Tabitha became ill one day and died. When her friends heard that Peter was visiting the nearby town of Lydda, they sent messengers to him, asking him to come at once.

Peter wasted no time. He hurried back with the messengers and they took him straight into Tabitha's house and upstairs to the room where her body had been laid out for burial. Around her bed were a number of widows, all weeping bitterly. They showed Peter some of the clothes Tabitha had generously made for them.

Peter sent all the mourners out of the room. Then he knelt down and prayed. After a while he turned to the bed and said, "Tabitha, stand up!"

Tabitha opened her eyes. She looked across at Peter and then sat up. Peter helped her to her feet, then he called her friends back into the room so that they could see she was alive again. They were overjoyed.

The whole of Jaffa heard the story of Tabitha, and through it many came to believe in Jesus.

Peter's vision

Peter stayed in Jaffa for some time, lodging at the house of a leather-tanner called Simon.

One day, he went up on to the flat roof to pray. Peter was feeling hungry at the time and looking forward to his lunch. Just then, he fell into a trance and saw a vision of heaven opening and a huge sheet being lowered towards him, filled with every possible kind of animal and bird.

A voice then said to him, "Now, Peter, kill something and eat it."

Peter was horrified. "No, Lord. I have never eaten anything unclean, or forbidden by the Law."

Then the voice said, "What God has made clean, you have no right to call unclean." Three times the voice said this. Then the sheet was drawn back up into heaven.

Peter was still puzzling over what the vision might mean, when the Holy Spirit spoke to him. "Hurry, some men have come to see you. Do not hesitate to travel back with them, for it was I that called them to you."

"We are servants of Cornelius, a Roman centurion," the visitors explained. "He is a good man, who worships the God of the Jews. He is highly regarded by the Jewish community in Caesarea. While he was praying, he had a vision of an angel that told him to send for you and to listen to what you have to say."

The next day, when Peter went with them to the house of Cornelius, he understood his own vision. "It would be wrong for me, a Jew, to enter the house of foreigners. But God has made it clear to me that I must not assume anyone is unclean or common. God does not have favourites. Anyone – of any nationality – who fears God and does what is right, is acceptable to him."

While Peter talked with Cornelius and his household, the Holy Spirit came down on them. Peter baptised them all and stayed with them several days.

Peter in prison

King Herod Agrippa now ruled over the Jews. He was a fierce enemy of the Christian church and had many of its followers executed, among them James, the brother of John. When he saw that this pleased the Jews, he arrested Peter as well.

Peter was kept heavily chained between two soldiers inside his prison cell, and four squads of soldiers took turns to guard his prison day and night. The church prayed for him continuously.

The night before his trial, an angel sent from God appeared in Peter's cell, filling it with light. He tapped Peter on the shoulder and told him to get up.

"Hurry!" said the angel, as the chains fell away from Peter's wrists. "Put on your belt and sandals. Wrap your cloak around you and follow me."

The angel led Peter past all the sleeping guards and right up to the prison gates which opened on their own. Peter could not believe it was really happening: he thought he was dreaming. Out in the city, they walked almost the length of one street before the angel left him. At that moment Peter came to his senses. "It's true," he thought. "God really did send his angel to save me from Herod."

Then he went straight to the house of Mary and her son, Mark, where a number of Christians were praying. They could not believe it was Peter at the door! Peter then told them all that had happened.

King Herod, in the meantime, was enraged to discover that his prisoner had disappeared, and in his fury had all the prison guards put to death.

Paul and Barnabas

Paul and Barnabas were teaching at Antioch, the third largest city in the Roman Empire at that time. The Holy Spirit directed them to undertake a special mission, so after fasting and praying they set off for Asia Minor – where the people believed in the mythical gods of the Greeks – stopping at various places on their journey to preach the Good News.

When they reached the town of Lystra they met a crippled man who had never been able to walk. He listened to Paul preaching and managed to catch his attention. Paul could see that the man had faith, so he said to him, "Get to your feet – stand up!" At once, the man stood up and walked.

The people of Lystra were astonished. "These are gods disguised as men!" they said, and began calling Barnabas "Zeus", and Paul "Hermes" since they thought he was the messenger of the gods. Hearing of the miracle, the local priests of Zeus brought an ox with a garland of flowers round its neck, intending to offer it as sacrifice for them both. Paul and Barnabas were horrified.

"Friends! What do you think you are doing?" cried Paul. "We are just men like yourselves, not gods. We have brought you the Good News of the one true God who made all things. He provides the rain and sun and brings you food and happiness. We beg you to turn away now from your empty idols."

Despite the anger of a group of Jews who tried to stone them, Paul and Barnabas made a number of new Christians in Lystra before continuing their journey.

Mark the helper

Paul and Barnabas took Barnabas' young nephew, Mark, with them on part of their first journey together. However, he only went as far as Pamphylia, and then turned back home to Jerusalem.

Mark may have been the young man who followed the disciples into the garden of Gethsemane when Jesus was arrested, since the incident only occurs in Mark's Gospel.

Barnabas wanted to take Mark along with them on another journey. But Paul would not hear of it. He was not going to take someone who deserted them the first time round! It was the cause of a great argument between them both, so that Paul and Barnabas split up and went different ways. Barnabas took Mark with him to Cyprus while Paul went off to Syria with a disciple called Silas.

We know that Mark made up for his early failings and eventually worked alongside Paul. Paul includes a greeting from Mark in his letter to the Colossians. "You were sent some instructions about him," he wrote. "If he comes to you, give him a warm welcome."

When Paul was a prisoner in Rome he put in his second letter to Timothy, "Get Mark to come and bring him with you; I find him a useful helper in my work."

Mark helped Peter, too. Peter was like a father to him and referred to Mark as his "son". And it was Mark who wrote the very first Gospel, setting down the Good News of Jesus for all to read.

Disagreement about the pagans

Paul and Barnabas returned to Antioch and related their adventures to the Christians there. Paul told them all how he had opened the door of faith to the pagans – that is, people who were not Jews.

This caused a few arguments between the disciples. Many thought that the pagans ought to become Jews before they were baptised as Christians. After all, Jesus was a Jew. It was decided that Paul and Barnabas should go back to Jerusalem to discuss this important matter with the apostles and elders of the church.

They were given a very warm welcome at Jerusalem and everyone was pleased to hear the news of all the new Christians they had made on their travels.

However, there was a group of believers who had at one time been Pharisees (very strict Jews). They insisted that pagan converts should become Jews and receive instruction in the Law of Moses. After a very long discussion, Peter stood up and addressed the assembly.

"My brothers, don't forget that God showed his approval of the pagans by giving them his Holy Spirit just as he did to us. God made no distinction between them and us, but purified their hearts by faith. Remember, we are all saved the same way: by the grace of Jesus Christ."

It was decided, then, not to put extra burden on new Christians from among the pagans, but to ask them to lead good lives and have nothing to do with pagan idols.

Silas is chosen

There was so much work to be done to spread the Good News that the apostles realised Paul and Barnabas would need some help in Antioch. They therefore chose two more disciples to go with them: Judas Barsabbas and Silas. Both men were fine speakers and already important members of the church.

The party set off for Antioch, taking with them a letter from the church in Jerusalem addressed to all the new Christians from amongst the pagans. It apologised for any distress which might have been caused by the disagreements amongst the brothers, outlined the way of life they were expected to lead, and introduced Judas and Silas who would be working with Barnabas and Paul.

Both Judas and Silas spoke at length to the community at Antioch, encouraging them and strengthening them in their faith. The Christians there were delighted.

When Paul and Barnabas eventually went their separate ways, Paul chose Silas to accompany him on his next journey. They set off for Syria and Cilicia, visiting all the communities of believers along the way, giving them help and encouragement.

Paul meets Timothy

From Cilicia, Paul and Silas visited Derbe and Lystra once again. This time, they met a young disciple in Lystra called Timothy, whose father was Greek. Timothy had come to believe in Jesus first through the faith of his grandmother, Lois, and then through the faith of his mother, Eunice; a Jewess who had become a Christian.

Paul prayed over Timothy and laid hands on him so he received the Holy Spirit. Then Paul had Timothy disguised as a Jew, to make it safer for him to travel and teach amongst the Jewish communities.

Over the years, Timothy was to become a very close companion to Paul, accompanying him on many of his missionary journeys. Paul referred to Timothy as "dear child of mine" and spoke of him with fatherly affection. Later, he left Timothy in charge of the church at Ephesus.

From Lystra, Paul and his companions continued visiting one town after another in Asia Minor, passing on the decisions made by the apostles and elders in Jerusalem to the pagans who wanted to follow Christ. As a result, the churches grew strong in faith and increased daily in their number of believers.

Then, one night Paul had a vision in which he saw a man from Macedonia who came and appealed to Paul saying, "Please come to Macedonia and help us!" Paul had no doubt that God was calling them to bring the Good News to the people of Macedonia, so they immmediately set off for the port of Troas.

A lady named Lydia

Paul and his companions sailed from Troas to the Roman city of Philippi – the largest city in that part of Macedonia. There was no synagogue here for the local Jewish community, so instead each Sabbath they used to gather together for prayers by the river outside the city gates.

Paul and his friends joined them in their worship, sitting down with the women and talking to them about Jesus. One of the women in the group was a very devout lady called Lydia. She was not from Philippi but Lydia worshipped the God of the Jews. She was a wealthy woman, with her own house and purple-dye business. At that time it was very expensive to produce the colour purple: it was therefore used only for the robes of very wealthy and high-ranking Romans, including the Emperor himself.

Lydia listened to Paul's teaching and the Holy Spirit opened her heart to believe in the Good News of Jesus. She and her household were all baptised into the Church.

Afterwards, Lydia sent Paul a message: "If you think I am a true believer in the Lord, please come and stay with us."

Since Lydia refused to accept any excuse, Paul and his companions did as she asked, and Lydia's house became not only home to the travellers, but also the first meeting place for the Christians in Philippi.

Paul and Silas in prison

Paul and his friends continued to spread the Good News in Philippi, until one day Paul healed a slave girl of madness. The girl's masters were furious, for they had made a great deal of money out of her ravings, using her to tell fortunes. They seized Paul and Silas and dragged them along to the law court held in the market place, accusing them of breaking the law.

The magistrates found the disciples guilty as charged and ordered them to be flogged and thrown into prison. Their jailer was told to keep a close eye on them, so he chained them to the wall of his most secure cell and fastened their feet in stocks.

Late into the night, the other prisoners could hear Paul and Silas singing and praising God. Suddenly a wild earth tremor shook the prison right down to its foundations. All the doors flew open and the chains fell from all the prisoners.

When the jailer woke and saw the prison doors flung wide, he was terrified that his prisoners had escaped. He drew his sword, intending to kill himself.

"Do not harm yourself!" shouted Paul. "We are all here!"

The jailer called for lights, and when he saw Paul and Silas he threw himself at their feet. "Sirs, what must I do to be saved?" he asked.

"Believe in the Lord Jesus," they told him, and explained the Good News of Jesus. That night the jailer and his household were all baptised. Paul and Silas went to the jailer's house for a meal and the whole family celebrated with them.

In the morning, the magistrates sent an order to the jail that Paul and Silas should be released.

Paul and the wise men of Athens

Because his life was in danger from the Jews, Paul had to flee to Athens, where he waited for Timothy and Silas to join him. He became very angry at the sight of all the statues and temples around the city, dedicated to different mythical gods. Every day they argued the matter in the synagogue and the market place. Some of his listeners made fun of him, but others invited Paul to address the council.

"Some of the things you say seem very strange to us," they said, "and we would like to know what they mean." Athenians loved to listen to a good talk.

"Men of Athens," began Paul as he stood in front of the entire council. "I see from your temples and statues that you are all very religious. In fact, I even saw one altar dedicated 'To an Unknown God'. Well, your unknown god is in fact the God I proclaim. So you worship him already! Since he is Lord of heaven and earth he does not live in shrines or temples made by human hands. Nor does he need anything from us – in fact it is he who gives us everything, even life itself. It is in him that we live and move and have our very existence. As your own writers have said, 'We are all his children.' So there is no reason to suppose he looks like anything made in gold, or silver, or carved by a human hand.

"God overlooked this kind of belief while we didn't know any different. But then he made himself known through a man sent to show us the way to salvation. And to prove it, he raised that man to life from death."

At this many of his audience burst out laughing. Some, however, wanted to hear more and several became followers of Christ before Paul left Athens.

Paul at Corinth

Paul made his way from Athens to Corinth, an important city that lay on the trade route from Rome to Asia Minor. It was the capital of the Roman province of Achaia and home of the Roman proconsul, Gallio, so it was an important centre for Paul's ministry.

There were a number of Jewish families living in Corinth who had been exiled from Rome, and once Silas and Timothy arrived from Macedonia, Paul spent most of his time visiting the synagogue and preaching the Good News of Jesus.

A number of the Jews turned against Paul and became unpleasant towards him, so he shook out his cloak at them and declared: "I've done my best to teach you. It's your own fault if you don't want to hear what I say. I can now go and preach to the pagans with a clear conscience!"

But the others received him well. A great many Corinthians who heard what Paul and his companions had to say became believers. And even the president of the synagogue and his whole household were baptised.

It was while Paul was in Corinth that God gave him great encouragement for his work. One night he spoke to Paul in a vision and said, "Do not be afraid to speak out for my sake, or allow anyone to stop you. I am with you. I have so many faithful believers in this city that no one will try to hurt you."

So Paul stayed in Corinth for eighteen months.

Paul the tent-maker

Paul came from the city of Tarsus, in Cilicia, an area famous for its goats. The goat hair was woven to make a very strong cloth, while the hide was used to make leather goods. It was customary for every Jewish boy to learn a trade – generally his father's – so that he could earn his living when he grew up. Paul was trained in tent-making.

When he arrived in Corinth, Paul met a Jew named Aquila. He and his wife, Priscilla, were both tent-makers and were amongst those who had been forced to leave Italy because of the Emperor's new law. They invited Paul to lodge with them, and he earned his keep by helping them with their work.

But the attacks from hostile Jews grew worse. One day, Paul was seized and taken before the proconsul Gallio. "This man had been persuading people to worship God in a way that breaks the law!" said his accusers.

Before Paul could say anything in his defence, the proconsul replied angrily, "Listen. If this was about some criminal act I would not hesitate to give it my attention. But if it's only quibbles about words, or names, to do with your own Jewish law, then you must deal with it yourselves. I have no intention of making any legal decisions about things like that."

The Jews were so angry that they turned on their own leader and beat him up on the very steps of the courthouse. Gallio ignored them.

After this, Paul stayed for a while, but eventually decided it was time for him to move on. He said goodbye to the brothers in Corinth and set sail for Syria. His friends Priscilla and Aquila went with him as far as Ephesus, where their house became the meeting place for the Christians there. Paul kept in touch with them, however, and included affectionate greetings to them at the end of some of his letters.

Paul at Ephesus

Paul travelled to Caesarea, Antioch and Phrygia, giving help and encouragement to the churches there, before returning to Ephesus.

Ephesus was a great Roman city in Asia, famous as a centre of learning, commerce and trade. It was home of poets, philosophers, artists, craftsmen and historians.

When Paul first arrived, he found a number of believers already in the city. He asked them if they had received the Holy Spirit when they were baptised.

"No," they said. "We were never told there was such a thing as a Holy Spirit."

"Then how were you baptised?" Paul asked them.

"We were baptised with John's baptism," they replied.

"John's baptism," said Paul, "was one of repentance. But John insisted that the people should believe in the one who came after him. That is, Jesus."

When the disciples heard this, they asked to be baptised in the name of the Lord Jesus. The moment Paul laid his hands on them, the Holy Spirit came down on them and they began to speak in different languages and to prophesy.

Paul stayed in Ephesus for over two years, preaching the gospel of Christ every day. First in the synagogue, and then, when the Jews began attacking his teaching, in the public lecture hall of Tyrannus. In this way, people from all over Asia – both Jews and Greeks – gradually came to hear the Good News.

The riot of the silversmiths

At the very heart of Ephesus was the magnificent temple dedicated to the goddess Diana. It was one of the great wonders of the ancient world and a great attraction for the many followers of the goddess, who flocked to Ephesus from far and wide to worship at her shrine. These pilgrims also liked to take home with them images of the shrine, crafted in silver. It provided the silversmiths of Ephesus with a fine living.

Since his arrival in Ephesus, Paul had been proclaiming the one, true God, and had taught that idols made by human hands were not gods. So many people had come to believe him that the silversmiths found their trade was falling away.

This made the silversmiths very angry. They started a riot against the Christians, stirring up the people and shouting, "Great is Diana of the Ephesians!"

Paul's friends advised him to stay in hiding, but two

of his followers were grabbed by the mob and taken to the great amphitheatre. For two hours the crowd screamed and shouted, until eventually the town clerk managed to get their attention.

"Citizens of Ephesus!" he cried. "There is no need for this kind of behaviour. If the silversmiths have a case against anyone, they must take it to the law court. But we shall all be in great trouble if the Roman authorities hear about this."

The people quietly returned to their homes.

Paul knew that the real target of their anger was himself, so he called a meeting of the disciples and told them he had decided he must move on. After giving them words of encouragement, he said goodbye and set off for Macedonia.

A life saved at Troas

Paul travelled through Macedonia and Greece accompanied by several friends, including Timothy. They came to the town of Troas, where they stayed for several days.

The night before Paul was due to leave Troas, they all met together for a special meal and Paul preached a sermon that went on well into the night.

In those early days the faithful had to meet wherever they could, since there were no churches built. On this occasion they were in an upstairs room lit by several candles. With all the people crowded inside to hear Paul preach, the room became very warm.

There was a young man amongst the listeners. He was sitting on the windowsill, where there was some cool air. But as Paul talked, so the young man became more and more drowsy. Eventually, he nodded off completely and fell out of the window. He struck the ground three floors below, and lay still.

Friends rushed down the stairs. When they reached the boy they found he was dead. Paul knelt down and held the boy to him, in his arms.

"There's no need to worry," he said. "There is still life in him." And to everyone's relief, the young man was taken home, alive.

Paul, meanwhile, returned to the upper room where he broke bread with the others and continued his talk until dawn, when it was time for him to leave.

Paul says goodbye to the Ephesians

Pentecost was approaching, and Paul was anxious to be in Jerusalem in time for the great feast.

In order to avoid going into Ephesus again, Paul arranged for all the elders of the church of Ephesus to meet him when his ship stopped at the port of Mitylene.

"You all know how I have served the Lord among you," said Paul, addressing them. "Bringing the Good News to Jews and Greeks alike, and urging everyone to believe in our Lord Jesus in spite of the sorrows and trials that I suffered because of the plots of the Jews.

"Now you see me already a prisoner in spirit. I am on my way to Jerusalem and have no idea what's going to happen, except that the Holy Spirit has already made it clear that imprisonment and suffering await me. I am not worried about my life: all that matters to me is that I finish the race and complete the works that the Lord Jesus has given me.

"Now, I am quite sure that I will not see any of you again. So look after the flock that God has entrusted to you, and feed his church which he bought with his own blood. Be on your guard against those who would harm you.

"I now commend you all to God."

Paul knelt down with them and prayed. They all wept and put their arms round him, saddened that they would not see him again. Then they helped him board his ship once more.

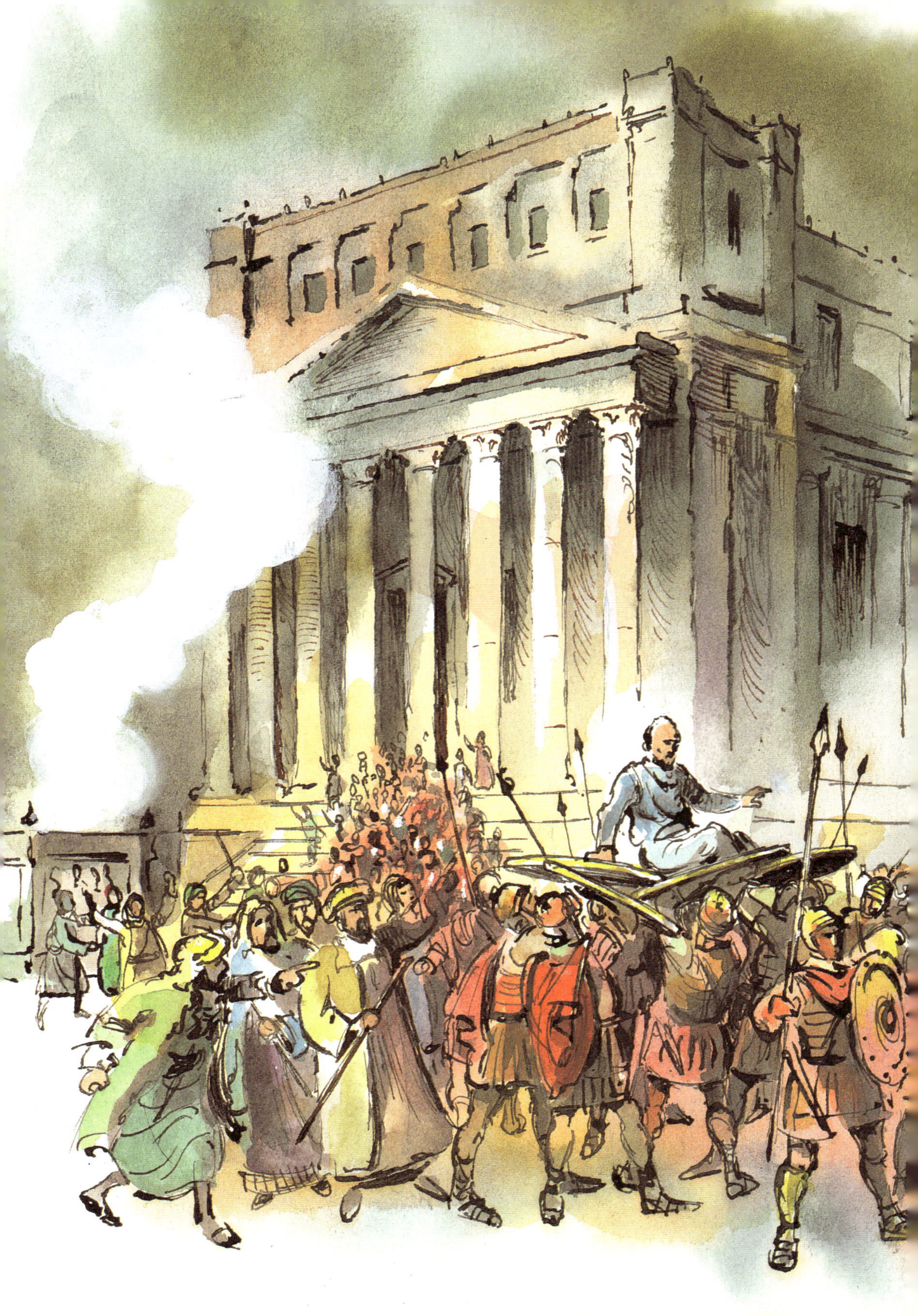

Paul in Jerusalem

When Paul arrived in Jerusalem the disciples were delighted to see him and hear his news, but they warned him that he had many enemies among the strict Jews in the city, who were accusing Paul of disregarding the law of Moses.

Paul went to the temple the very next day to show he was still a loyal Jew, but his enemies recognised him. "This is the man who has spoken against the law!" they cried, and suddenly there was uproar as crowds of people surged into the temple and dragged Paul outside.

News of the disturbance reached the commander of the Roman garrison, and he immediately sent out a company of soldiers to break up the mob. Paul was arrested and bound with chains. The only way through the crowd was for the soldiers to carry Paul to safety.

The next day, the commander summoned the Jewish council to find out exactly what charge they wanted brought against Paul.

Paul saved by a boy

That night, in the prison, the Lord appeared to Paul and said, "Courage! You have spoken up for me in Jerusalem. Now you must do the same in Rome."

Next day, a group of Jews made a solemn promise not to eat or drink until they had killed Paul. They went to the Jewish leaders and told them their plan.

"You must send a message to the commander of the garrison. Ask him to bring Paul out to you, so that you can ask him further questions. Then we will ambush the guard and get rid of Paul before he reaches you."

They didn't know that they had been overheard by the son of Paul's sister. The boy hurried to the garrison and told his uncle about the plot to kill him. Paul called a centurion: "Take this lad to the commander. He has something important to tell him."

The commander took the boy by the hand to a quiet corner where they would not be overheard. "What is it you have to tell me?" he asked him kindly.

The boy told him everything he had heard.

"Do not tell anyone else what you have told me," the commander warned him, and sent him home. Then he immediately gave orders for Paul to be taken to the Roman governor at Caesarea. He quickly wrote a letter for the governor, detailing the whole of Paul's case and warning him of the conspiracy against Paul.

That same night, Paul left Jerusalem and with him went an armed escort of four hundred infantry and seventy cavalry.

Paul a prisoner in Caesarea

Felix, the Roman governor at Caesarea, kept Paul a prisoner for two years. During that time Paul was free to be visited by his friends and receive anything he needed. Felix sent for Paul frequently, pretending to be interested in what Paul had to say, but really he hoped Paul would pay him money for his freedom.

After this, a new governor was appointed: a man called Festus. He was anxious to keep the peace with the Jews, so he continued to keep Paul a prisoner and summoned the chief priests from Jerusalem to state their case against Paul. They made many serious charges against Paul, but they did not have any evidence to prove them.

"I have not committed any offence against Jewish law, or the temple, or Caesar!" said Paul, in his defence.

"Would you be willing to go back to Jerusalem to face these charges before me there?" asked the governor.

Now Paul was a Roman citizen – a status which gave him a number of privileges. It was his right to bring his case before the Emperor, Caesar himself, if he chose to.

"If I have in fact committed any serious crime," he replied to Festus, "I would certainly accept even the death penalty. But I have done nothing wrong. Therefore I appeal to Caesar."

Festus discussed Paul's answer with his advisors, and seeing he had no other option said, "Very well. You have appealed to Caesar; to Caesar you shall go!"

Paul is brought before King Agrippa

Some days later, King Herod Agrippa paid a visit to Caesarea with his mother, Bernice. Festus told him all about Paul, and the king was keen to meet him for himself.

The very next day, Paul was brought before him and the king invited Paul to speak on his own behalf.

"King Agrippa, I am very honoured you have agreed to see me," said Paul. "I know you are an expert regarding Jewish matters, so I hope you will listen patiently to what I have to tell you."

Beginning with his early life, Paul told the king everything that had happened to him and why he thought the Jews were now trying to kill him.

Festus couldn't believe the things Paul was saying. "You are mad!" he cried, and tried to stop Paul speaking.

"I am not mad, your Excellency," Paul replied. "I am speaking nothing but the truth. The king knows that I have been frank and honest at all times. I know he believes in the prophets."

"A little more and you would have me a Christian," remarked the king, drily.

"Little or more," said Paul, "I wish before God that not only you but all who have heard me this day could come to be as I am – but without the chains!"

After discussion amongst his advisors, King Agrippa agreed that Paul should go to Rome. "If he had not appealed to Caesar, we could have set him free," he said. "He has done nothing that deserves death or imprisonment."

Paul sails for Rome

Paul was put in the charge of a Roman centurion, called Julius, for his voyage to Rome. He and some other prisoners went aboard a ship bound for several ports along the coast. With Paul were two of his companions. One of them was Luke, a doctor, who had joined the apostle at Troas and who later wrote of Paul's travels in the Acts of the Apostles. He also wrote one of the Gospels.

On their second day at sea they stopped at the port of Sidon. Julius kindly allowed Paul to go ashore and stay with friends while the ship was docked.

Then they sailed on towards Cyprus, but because the wind was blowing against them the ship took two weeks to reach Myra, its next port of call. Here, Julius found them a ship carrying grain to take them to Italy, but strong winds forced the captain to change their course and head for the island of Crete. They just managed to reach the Bay of Fair Havens, where they sheltered from the bad weather.

It was now late September and they had lost a great deal of time. Julius and the ship's captain discussed what they should do. Should they stay where they were, or try to reach the larger port of Phoenix, which was further round the coast?

Paul warned them of the dangers ahead. "We run the risk of not only losing the cargo and the ship, but also our lives!" he said.

In the end, it was decided they should continue to Phoenix, hoping they could spend the winter there. As they left the harbour of Fair Havens, a warm, southerly breeze sprang up, giving everyone new hope. It now seemed as if they would soon reach Phoenix safely, so they sailed closer to the coastline.

But as they continued to sail round the Cretan coast, a hurricane suddenly swept down on them from the north-east. The ship was tossed helplessly in the gale-force winds.

As well as the storm itself, the ship faced additional hazards from its cargo. As the grain became soaked by water, it would swell and burst the ship's timbers apart.

Storm at sea

Luke described what happened next: "Our ship was caught and could not be turned into the wind, so we just had to give in and allow the storm to take it. We were swept dangerously towards the lee shore of a small island. The crew managed to strengthen the ship by passing heavy cables right around it, then they floated out the sea anchor to help prevent the ship from being driven ashore. Unable to steer, they just had to let the ship drift.

"The next day the weather was no better. The ship could not stand the heavy battering of the storm and the waves, so the sailors had to start throwing some of the cargo overboard.

"On the third day, the crew had to jettison the ship's gear.

"For days the storm raged. The sky and sea were black, so neither sun nor stars were visible. We had no idea where we were and finally we gave up all hope of surviving."

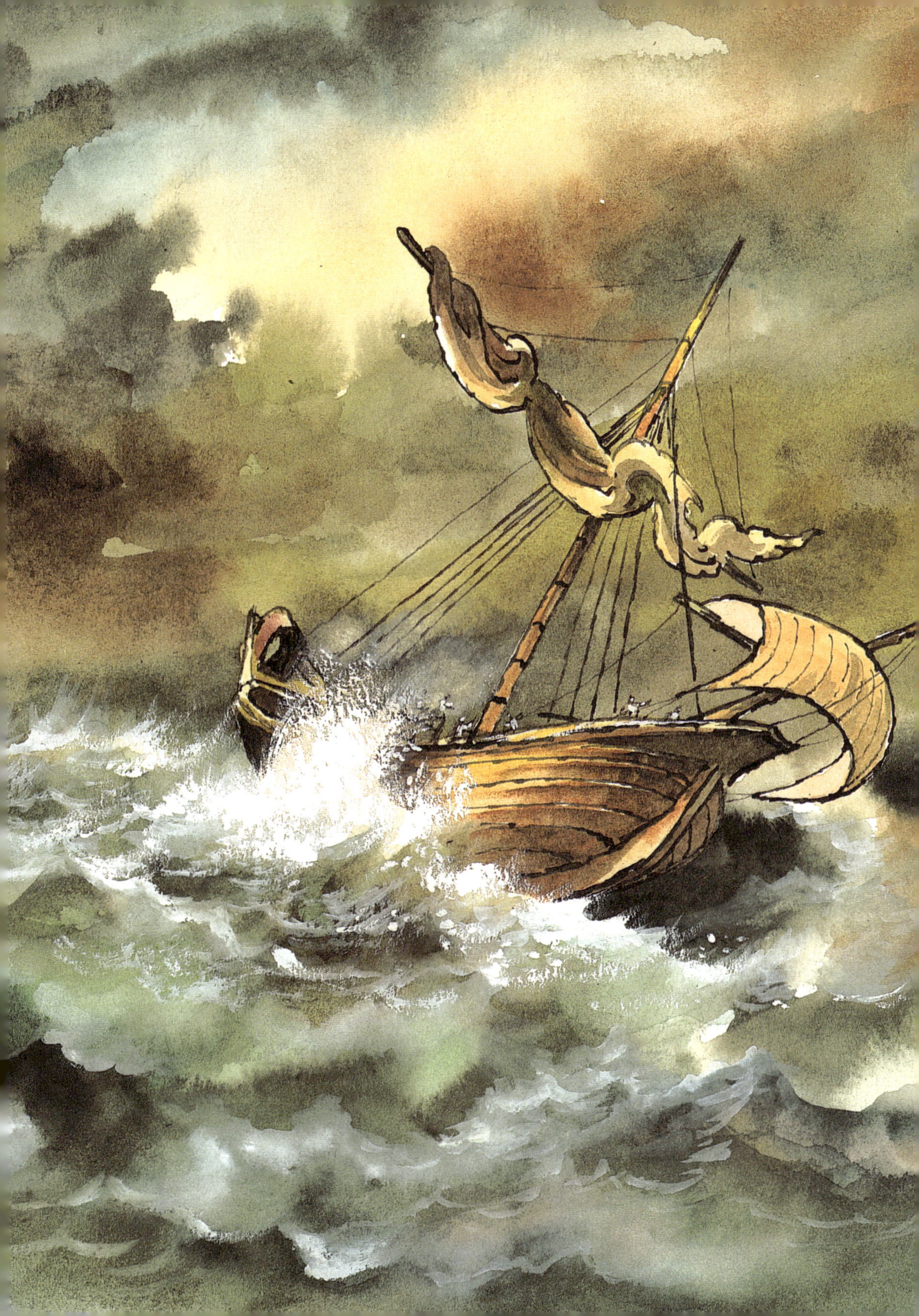

Paul gives everyone hope

It was then that Paul stood up and addressed them. "Friends," he said. "If you had listened to me and not sailed on for Phoenix we would not now be in this mess. But now I ask you not to give up hope. None of us will die, but we will lose the ship. Last night an angel came from the God I serve, and told me not to be afraid. 'You are destined to appear before Caesar,' he said, 'and for this reason God will keep you and all those who travel with you, safe.' So take courage, friends. God will look after us."

After two weeks at sea, the sailors at last saw signs of land. It was dark, so to prevent the ship running aground, they made frequent checks of the depth of the sea and secured four anchors from the stern.

But some of the sailors were so frightened they tried to lower the boat, to escape. Paul warned Julius, "Unless those men remain aboard, we will not survive." So the centurion and his men cut the boat adrift.

With dawn approaching, Paul assured everyone that their safety was in no doubt. But they needed to eat. He took a crust of bread from his bag, gave thanks to God and encouraged the others to eat as well. All two hundred and seventy-six passengers and crew ate as much as they wanted.

By now it was light enough for them to see that the ship had drifted towards a rocky creek with a small beach where they could run the ship aground.

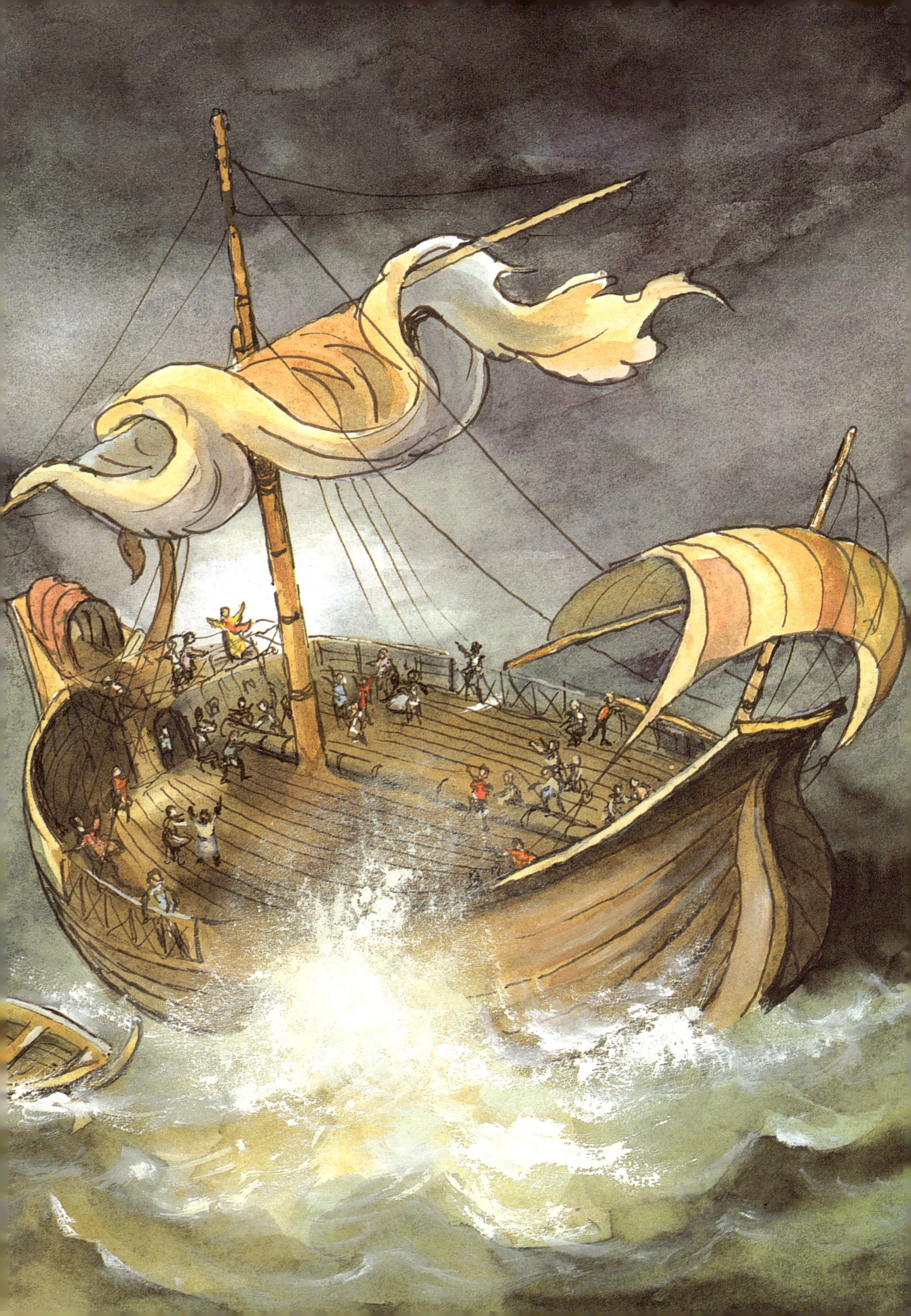

Shipwreck

Now that they had eaten and Paul had given them all fresh courage with his confident reassurance they would be safe, the sailors threw the remaining grain cargo into the sea, to lighten the ship. In the poor light of the stormy morning, they couldn't see much of the land they had reached, but they were able to see a rocky creek, so they made preparations to run the ship aground on the small beach.

They cut away the stern anchors and loosened the ropes they had tied round the rudder to secure it when the storm first struck. Then they raised the foresail into the wind. Free of its cargo and gear, the ship caught the wind and surged towards the beach.

Unfortunately, the sailors were unaware of the strong cross-currents in the coastal waters here. The ship was picked up by these currents and carried right on to a shoal of rocks. The bows of the vessel stuck fast between the rocks, while waves pounded the stern until it began to break up. It was time to abandon ship.

The Roman soldiers wanted to kill all the prisoners on board, to make sure they didn't swim off and escape. But their officer, Julius, would not let them. He was determined to deliver Paul safely to Rome, so he gave the order that everyone who could swim should do so and make their way to shore first, while the others should follow, using pieces of wreckage from the ship to keep them afloat.

In this way, everyone on board made it safely ashore, just as Paul had promised they would.

It was then they made the discovery that they had arrived on the island of Malta, situated between Sicily and North Africa.

Paul on the island of Malta

It was cold and raining when the survivors came ashore. At once they began to build a large fire, with the help of the local people who showed them all great kindness. Paul gathered a bundle of sticks, too, and was just putting them on the fire when a poisonous snake suddenly emerged from the wood and sank its fangs into his hand.

The islanders watched, horrified, expecting Paul to swell up or drop dead. But when he simply shook off the snake and remained unharmed, they were convinced Paul must be a god.

Paul and his two companions were invited up to the house of the governor of the island, a man called Publius. He made them feel very welcome and they stayed with him for three days. While they were there, they discovered that the father of Publius was very ill with a fever. Paul went to see him. He prayed at the man's bedside, laid his hands on the man and healed him.

News of the miracle quickly spread across the island, so that other sick people came to Paul to be healed, too.

"The islanders honoured us with many gifts," commented Luke, "and when it was time for us to leave, they brought on board all the provisions we could possibly want."

After three months, they set sail once more in an Alexandrian merchant ship that had spent the winter sheltering in Malta.

Paul comes to Rome

They left Malta and sailed to Syracuse, in Sicily, where they stayed for three days before continuing up the coast to Rhegium, on the southern tip of Italy.

Here the ship picked up a warm, southerly wind that took them quickly to their destination port of Puteoli, where Paul and his companions stayed with the Christian community for a week.

From Puteoli they travelled north overland, along the Appian Way to Rome. News of Paul's coming had already reached the Christian brotherhood in Rome, and some of the brothers came out to meet him. After his tiring journey, their warm welcome put new heart into Paul and he thanked God for them.

And so at long last Julius delivered Paul safely into Rome. It would take some time before his appeal to the Emperor could be arranged, and in the meantime he was allowed to stay in his own private lodgings, which he paid for himself. But there was always a Roman soldier guarding him at all times.

Paul remained under house arrest for two years. During that time he was always busy and kept in touch with the other churches he had helped set up, receiving visitors from far and wide, and continuing to teach the truth about Jesus. In particular, he was able to write or dictate long letters to various churches and brothers in Christ, and some of these have survived to form part of the New Testament.

Paul contacts the Jews of Rome

Paul had only been in Rome for three days when he invited all the senior Jews in Rome to come and visit him. He then explained to them why he was there.

"Although I have done nothing wrong against our people or the customs of our ancestors," he said, "I was arrested in Jerusalem and handed over to the Romans. They could not find me guilty of anything that deserved the death penalty, and would have set me free, but the Jews objected and I was forced to appeal to Caesar. I have asked you to come and see me so I could make it clear why it is I am a prisoner."

"We've had no letters about you from Judaea," they replied. "We'd like you to tell us in your own words about the Way you follow, so that we can make up our own minds about it."

And so they arranged to visit Paul again. This time, a large number of them crowded into his lodging to hear what he had to say.

Paul put his case to them, telling them about Jesus, their true Messiah, and giving evidence from the Law of Moses and the prophets. All day – from morning until evening – they discussed and argued the matter. Some were persuaded and believed, but most did not. As they took their leave, Paul sighed and told them, "You must understand that, since you do not want to believe, God's salvation has been sent to the pagans. And they will listen to it."

A runaway slave

While Paul was in Rome he met a young runaway slave called Onesimus. The name meant "useful". In those days richer Roman households usually had a number of slaves to look after the house and do menial jobs. By running away, Onesimus faced the possibility of painful maiming, branding or even death if he was caught.

Paul taught Onesimus about Jesus, and how he forgives all those who are truly sorry for the things they have done wrong. Onesimus became a Christian and stayed with Paul, looking after the apostle during his imprisonment. But Onesimus knew he would have to go back to his master one day and face his punishment.

Paul happened to discover that the owner of Onesimus was a man called Philemon. Now, it was through Paul that Philemon had become a Christian. His house was the meeting place for the church where he lived.

"I'm writing to you from prison," Paul wrote to Philemon, "to ask you to welcome someone you probably thought you'd never see again: your slave, Onesimus. You might have thought him useless once, but he is now a Christian and your brother in the Lord. I should like to keep him with me, but only with your consent. Please welcome him as you would welcome me, and if he owes you any money I will repay it."

Paul ended his letter with the hope that he would soon be out of prison and able to come and stay with Philemon once again.

The Roman soldier

Paul would sometimes use everyday images in his letters to help his readers understand the point he was making. In his letter to the church at Ephesus, for instance, he used the example of the Roman soldier to urge the church members to "grow strong in the Lord."

The Roman Empire brought peace, law and order to the lands it conquered. Battalions of highly-trained, professional soldiers made sure that law and order were maintained. So the image of the well-disciplined soldier wearing helmet and armour, and carrying a short sword or spear and shield, became familiar to everyone.

Paul himself travelled to Rome in the company of the centurion, Julius. And in Rome there was always a soldier on guard at Paul's lodgings.

"Put God's armour on," says Paul to the Ephesians, "so as to resist the attacks of the enemy. Stand your ground, with truth as a belt round your waist, and honesty as your breastplate. Wear your willingness to spread the Good News as shoes on your feet and always carry the shield of faith to protect you from the flaming arrows of the evil one. Your helmet is the salvation of God, and your sword the gift of the Word of God from the Spirit.

"Pray all the time for the things you need. And pray for me to be given the opportunity to speak without fear and proclaim the Gospel, of which I am an ambassador in chains."

203

Faithful to the end

One of the last letters that Paul wrote was to Timothy, who became one of the leaders of the early church and whom Paul loved as a son.

Paul gave a great deal of advice and encouragement to Timothy, for he knew that his own life was drawing to a close, and he was anxious that Timothy should not grow discouraged during the difficult times ahead. There were people in Rome working against Paul, and when he attended his first defence hearing, all the witnesses who had promised to give evidence for him failed to turn up.

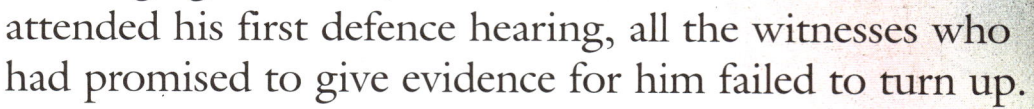

"Be careful always to choose the right course," wrote Paul. "Be brave under trial. Make the proclaiming of the Good News your life's work."

"As for me," he continued, "my life is already being poured away as an offering, and the time has come for me to be gone. I have fought the good fight to the end; I have run the race to the finish; I have kept the faith. All there is to come now is the crown of righteousness reserved for me, which the Lord, the righteous judge, will give me on that Day – and not only to me, but to all those who have longed for him.

"The Lord will rescue me from all evil and bring me safely to his heavenly kingdom. To him be glory for ever and ever. Amen."

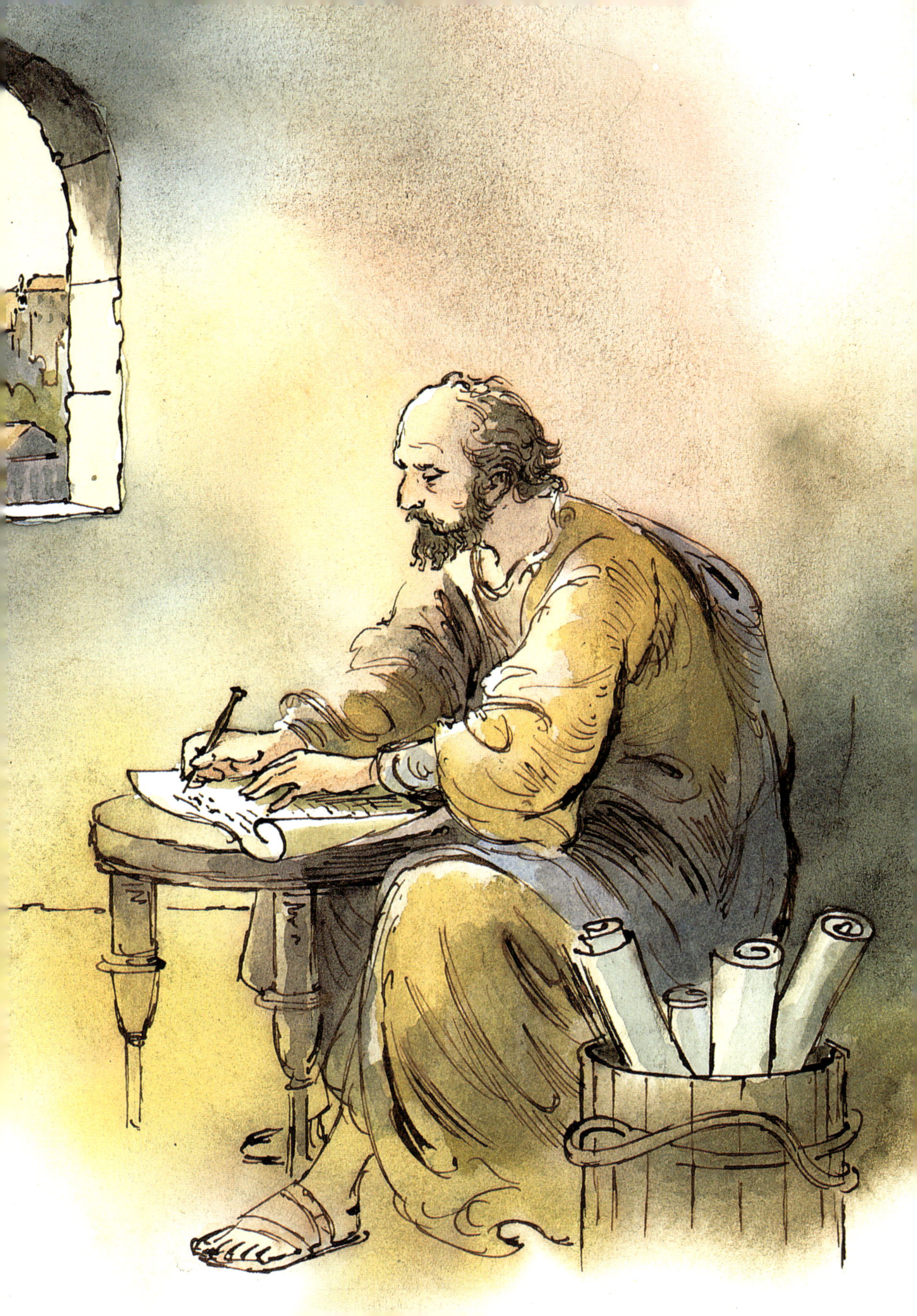

PANNONIA
ITALY
Rome
ILLYRICUM
MACEDONIA
Puteoli
Philip
Thessalonica
GREECE
Athens
SICILY
Corinth
Carthage
Syracuse
MALTA
MEDITERRANEAN
CYRENAICA
AFRICA

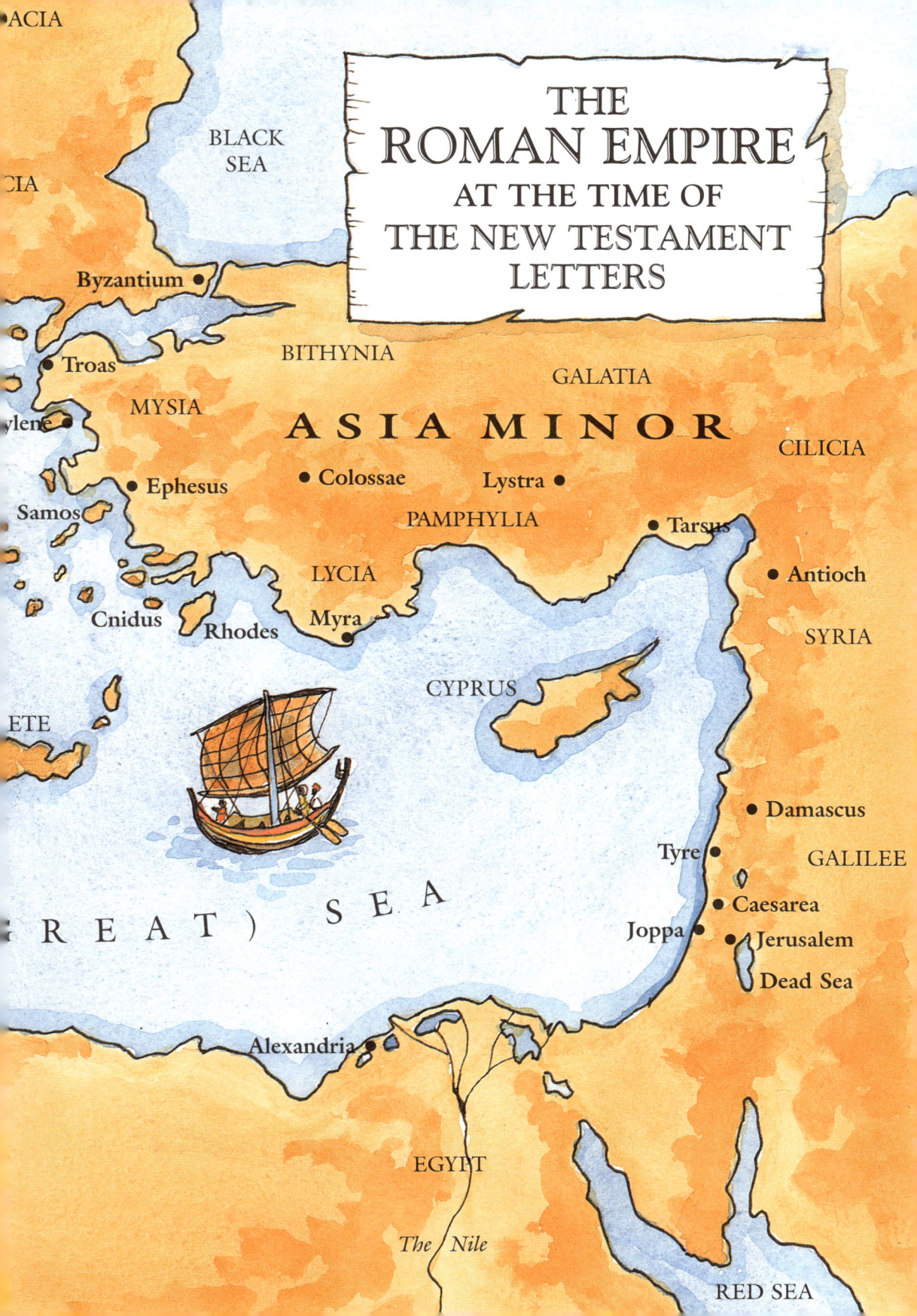

THE ROMAN EMPIRE AT THE TIME OF THE NEW TESTAMENT LETTERS